SOMETHING REAL

WHISKEY MEN

BOOK TWO

HOPE FORD

Something Real © 2023 by Hope Ford

Editor: Kasi Alexander

Cover Design: Lori Jackson

Cover Model: Wander Aguiar and Cass

Image Photographer: Wander Aguiar Photography

LILIAN

I wipe at the tears in the corner of my eyes. I've held it together for as long as I can, but it seems to be catching up with me now. It could be because I've been busy most of the day and haven't had time to really think about things. But what can I say? I knew that I wasn't going to be able to keep the emotions in forever. It's not every day that your baby sister, the one you've raised since she turned eleven, gets married.

I watch as Carrie walks around the reception, hugging people, laughing, and smiling ear to ear. Her husband, Phillip, is a good man, and I'm so glad that they found each other. She was a freshman in college when he was in his fourth and final year at the same university. They dated for four years, and as soon as she graduated, he proposed. After that, everything went by super fast. We planned a wedding. We moved all of her things into his house last week, they got married today, and tonight will be her first night in her new home with her new husband.

I thought I was ready for all this, but obviously it's going to take me some time to adjust.

Carrie and Phillip have a way about them that sort of makes me envious. He walks around the room with her, keeping a protective hand on her but also letting her stand out and be the exuberant woman that she is. Randomly, he reaches out to kiss her, and she smiles up at him.

I have to force myself to look away because it somehow feels like I'm butting in on a private moment between them.

I nod my head at my date, who's standing a few feet away. He's enjoying a second round at the buffet, and the way he's smiling I know that he's thinking this is more than it is. I'm going to feel bad if I hurt his feelings when I tell him we can't go out again. I probably should have thought about that before I asked him to be my date. I'm going to blame Carrie for that one.

I take a sip of my champagne and let the fruity taste tingle its way down my throat. I look out at the party and don't recognize a lot of people. Unfortunately, Carrie and I don't have any family, and we only have a few close friends here. The majority of the people are from Phillip's side of the family, but I love watching as they all hug and love on Carrie. She deserves to be a part of a big family.

I try not to feel down or that I'm being left behind. I know my sister loves me.

As if she can hear my thoughts, she turns to look at me, and I push my feelings to the side as I smile at her. She hugs her husband, whispers something to him, and then makes her way over to me.

Just watching her walk across the room brings back all the memories of the last twelve years together. Holding her in my arms when I told her our parents were killed in an automobile accident, helping her navigate puberty, high school, her first boyfriend and heartbreak. The day she graduated from high school. When she got accepted to Jasper University. The day she came home and told me she'd found the man she was going to marry, her college graduation, and then today when I helped her put her veil on before walking with her down the aisle to her husband. We've practically grown up together because at eighteen, I wasn't ready for all of this.

She stops and points at me. "What's that look?"

I sniff and shrug my shoulders, acting as if I don't

have a clue what she's thinking about. "What look?" I finish my drink and set it on the tray of a server passing by. "Oh you mean the look that says *finally, I get the house to myself. Finally!*"

She doesn't laugh. Instead, she looks at me worriedly. "Are you going to be okay? I mean, you're going to be at the house... by yourself."

I laugh it off even though she's putting voice to exactly what I was thinking last night in bed, mentally preparing myself for today. "Yes, I'm going to be all right. Of course, I am. As a matter of fact, you may want to call before you come over because I may be having a dinner party, or entertaining... or, or something."

Carrie reaches over and wraps her hand around mine. "Stop it, sis. I'm being serious. You've never been on your own before. I'm going to feel bad, leaving you to your puzzles and reality television."

I try to hold back the grimace. I knew I should have tried harder to pay for her to live on campus the last four years. Instead, she was home with me and saw my sad nightly ritual of watching reality television while doing puzzles. It has a lot to do with the fact that there was never extra money for going out, traveling, or shopping. Nope, the last twelve years have been spent on raising Carrie, her therapy, and putting her through school. The fact she's graduated with no debt was something I really wanted for her, and at least I was able to make that happen.

"First of all, you enjoyed the trashy television and puzzle nights just as much as I did, and don't act like you didn't. But really, you don't have to worry about me. I'm going to be fine."

Did my voice break as I said it? I feel my eyes widen, knowing it did.

She grabs my other hand and holds them both between us. "Listen to me, sis. For the last twelve years, you have completely dedicated your life to me." I start to interrupt her, but she shakes her head. "No, don't even try to act like you didn't because we both know it's the truth. And now, I'm okay. I need you to know that I'm good. I finished school, I'm married, I'm starting a teaching job at the beginning of next semester, and I'm good now." She points at herself and her husband across the room. "I know that everything I have, everything I am is because of you. I owe you so much."

I do stop her this time. "No, don't say that. You don't owe me anything. I love you, Carrie."

She nods and releases my hand as she wipes at a tear on her cheek. She laughs as she wipes it away, being careful not to smear any makeup. "I told myself I wasn't going to cry today, but I should have known I wouldn't get through this conversation without it." She takes a deep breath and lets it out slowly. "I love you, too. And that's why I need you to do something for me."

I don't even hesitate. "Anything, you know that."

She nods. "I need you to live it up, Lilian. I want you to go out, take photography courses, travel, go on dates, be happy. You grew up too fast, and you had to because of me." I open my mouth, but she shakes her head, rolls her eyes, and holds her hand up all at the same time. It's something she mastered around the age of fifteen. "I'm serious, Lilian. You deserve happiness, and you deserve to be loved and love someone else. You deserve everything. Can you do this for me?"

I wrap my arms around her neck, pulling her into me. "I promise, kiddo."

She grabs my upper arms and pushes away from me. "I'm serious. Don't think you can just tell me okay and I'm going to forget about it. I'm not letting this go."

I blow out a breath. "I got it. Date, live it up, sleep around, travel..."

I trail off on my list as she starts to laugh. "I never said sleep around. I mean, good for you, add that one on there, but we can both see where your mind's at."

She looks over at my date, who is sitting at the table eating and playing on his phone. "So you and Victor..."

I put my arm around her waist. "No, not me and Victor... he's my date. That's it. You told me I had to bring a date, so I brought one."

Again with the eye rolling. "I didn't mean with the first guy that asked you out."

I pinch her side. "He's been asking me out since I started at Blaze Whiskey two years ago, and what's wrong with him? He's nice."

She nods, eyes wide and innocent. "Yes, yes, he is nice. But he doesn't look like the type that's going to take control in the bedroom or take you to the promised land if you know what I mean."

I cover my hands over my ears. "Blah, blah, blah... I don't want to hear it. To me, you're still the eleven-year-old girl that I had to lie down in bed with to get you to go to sleep. I don't want to hear you talking about s-e-x."

Her mouth falls open. "Did you just spell it? Lilian, you're thirty years old. Geez, you do need to get laid."

I cover her mouth because of course by the end of the sentence her voice raises, and everyone around is staring at us. "Are you serious right now?"

She pulls away from me. "I love you, sis. Don't forget what you promised me." I watch as she practically floats across the room to her husband. He opens his arms to her when she gets close, and they embrace.

I motion to the bartender for another drink. I'm going to need one after that conversation.

FORD

"**D**id you remember your lunch box today?"

Ollie groans from the back seat. "Yes, I have my lunch box and backpack. I have it all, Dad."

I laugh as I look at him through the rearview mirror. He seems surprised that I would ask him when in fact he forgets things on the regular. I glance at him again, expecting to see him rolling his eyes or something, but I'm surprised when I see the pensive look on his face. "What's wrong?" I ask instantly.

He lifts his head to look at me, and I catch the grief that's still in his eyes before I have to force myself to look at the road in front of me. My voice softens. "What is it, Ollie? Something bothering you?"

"I was just thinking about Granny, that's all."

I nod my head and try to tamp down the emotion that wells up every time I think about my grandmother. She was Ollie's great-grandmother, and they had a really good relationship with each other. I know he's missing her. Hell, we all feel sort of lost without her. But it's only been a few months; I'm hoping with time, this gets easier for him. "I know, bub. I still think about her all the time too. But remember what we talked about, no matter what, Granny will always be with you."

He lets out a loud, dramatic sigh. "I know. But she always made my birthday special. She would make cupcakes with me and then bring them to school for a party." He turns to look out the window. "I guess I just won't have a party at school this year."

My hands clench on the steering wheel. Damn it, I didn't even think of that. Usually, Granny would come over and she and Ollie would make an absolute disaster of my kitchen, making cupcakes. She always did the party thing at the school. That was their thing. How could I have forgotten that?

I pull into the line at the school, and it's slow moving to the front. "Ollie."

He doesn't look at me, and I say his name again. "Ollie, look at me."

He finally pulls his eyes off the window and looks

at me with a little bit of defiance. He's only five—soon to be six—and he's already strong minded. "How about you and I make the cupcakes and I'll bring them to school? You know, Granny taught me everything she knows... and I have her recipe for the icing you like."

He nods his head, but he doesn't seem excited like I hoped he'd be. "Yeah, sure, Dad. Sounds good."

I put my foot on the gas and move a little farther in the line. I had hoped that would have cheered him up, but it didn't. The kid has been through so much, first with his mom leaving after our divorce and never coming to see him. It's not like he knew her; she never spent any time with him before that, but still I know not having a mom bothers him sometimes. And then his Granny, the most important woman in his life, died, and it's a lot for me to deal with. I can just imagine how it affects a five-year-old.

We get to the very front of the line, and Ollie's unbuckling his belt. I need to see him smile before he gets out of this car. I need to know he's going to be okay, and I know this might not be the answer, but I'll try anything. "Besides the classroom party, how about we have a real party too? We can invite your friends, have pizza, presents... you love the trampoline park. We can do it there!"

I hold my breath when I think about what the soccer coach is going to have to say about the team going to the trampoline park. It's a broken ankle just waiting to happen, but I'm not going to worry about that now because my son's whole face is lighting up. "Really? Really, Dad? Can we?"

I nod enthusiastically. "Of course we can, buddy."

He lets out a "Whooo!" and dives to the front seat, wrapping his arms around my neck. "Thank you, Dad! I can't wait to tell my friends."

He releases me and he is back in his seat and opening his door before I can say anything but "I love you" to him. He's waving at me as he runs to the school. I'm not really sure what all has happened here. I'm already regretting it because I know I'm going to have to deal with his friends' moms that are getting more and more brazen.

At the honk of a horn, I throw my hand up in a wave and pull away from the curb. I can't take it back now, nor do I want to. I can deal with a few women flirting with me if it makes my kid happy. With that settled, I make a list in my head of everything I need to do for the party as I drive to work.

As I pull into Blaze Whiskey, the company I own with my brothers, I pull out my phone to call the trampoline park. The screen is locked, and I can't get it to do anything. I nod my head at a few people as I walk in, and when I get to my assistant's desk, I hand her my phone. She laughs. "What did you do this time?"

Her blond hair is curling around her face. She doesn't even have to stand up for me to know that she's wearing the black pencil skirt that makes grown men drool and her black high heels that show off her toned legs. Nope, any time she has on the blue button-down blouse that is a perfect match to her sky-blue eyes, that's what she wears with it. And usually by the end of the day, I have a bad case of blue balls, and I'm completely out of patience.

She's looking up at me expectantly, and I try to rein in my thoughts. "Uh, yeah, I'm not sure. It's just frozen."

She pushes some buttons on the side of the phone. "Did you try shutting it off and turning it back on again?"

I drag my eyes off the hint of cleavage before meeting her eyes. "Nope."

She does a few other things and hands back the phone. "There you go. Good as new."

"Thanks, Lilian. Do you think you can book the trampoline park for Ollie's party the weekend after his birthday? I imagine weekends book up pretty fast, so just see what you can do."

"Sure thing. I can't believe he's going to be six already. They sure do grow up fast."

I tap a hand on her desk, and for the first time, I notice her tired eyes. "How did the wedding go?"

She smiles. "It was beautiful. Everything went off without a hitch. Carrie was so happy."

Before I can ask her anything more, Victor from Accounting cuts the corner. He seems like a man on a mission until he sees me standing here. His steps slow, and he looks between Lilian and me. I should probably go on into my office, but I stand here, watching it all unfold.

"Hello, Mr. Blaze...uh, Ford."

"Hey there, Victor," I say to him easily.

The man gulps and looks at Lilian. "I really enjoyed going to the wedding with you... I mean, I had a really good time. I know." He pauses and looks at me, probably wishing for me to leave, but I'm not leaving because from what I just heard, he's making it sound like he went on a date with Lilian. But that can't be. Lilian doesn't date.

Victor pauses so long that Lilian waves her hand in front of his face. "Victor... you were saying?"

He tucks his arms across his chest. "Right. Uh, I had a good time. I know you said we are better off as friends, but I just thought I'd tell you that if you ever need a date for another family function, I'm your man."

Lilian smiles at Victor, and I'm not going to lie, it makes me angry. Her voice is super sweet when she answers him, which pisses me off more. "Thanks, Victor. I really appreciate that, but I don't have any more family to have functions... I mean, there's not any more parties in the foreseeable future."

I take a deep breath and try to keep the menacing tone out of my voice. "Lilian, can I see you in my office please?"

I don't wait for her answer, and with a dismissive stare toward Victor, I go into my office. I pace back and forth across the room before settling heavily behind my desk. What the actual fuck? She went on a date with Victor?

My stomach clenches, and I feel like I might pass out. Lilian walks into my office with a pad and pencil in her hand.

She sits down in the seat across from my desk and holds up her pen to start writing. "I'm ready."

She's looking at the paper, and I don't know what to say. I should focus on work, but the words come out of my mouth before I can stop them. "You're dating Victor?"

She seems surprised. I'm sure she thought I asked

her in here to take notes... not to butt into her personal life. "No, we went on one date."

I wave my hand, dismissing the semantics. "I thought you had some kind of rule about no dating."

She laughs, uncrosses her legs, and then crosses them again. "I do. I mean I did. Raising Carrie, putting her through school and college, I didn't have time to date. I was focused on her. But she was worried about me. She thinks I've given up on my dreams, and she's blaming herself." She shrugs uncomfortably. "She wants me happy."

I raise up from my seat and move around to sit on the edge of my desk. "And what? She thinks Victor will make you happy?"

"No, I mean, I uh, never brought guys home. She thinks I have some wild oats to sew or something."

Her face is red when she realizes what she just confessed. "Do you?" I ask her.

She shrugs. "No, I don't regret anything. I'm happy with where Carrie's at, but yeah, I'm looking forward to dating again. No strings. Just having a good time."

I try to keep myself calm, but she's basically just admitted that she's going to start dating. Since she started working here, two years ago, I've kept my distance. I hired her without any experience, but I knew that day that I wanted her near me. I was willing to settle for subpar work just to be near her. But she was a fast learner and spent plenty of her free time scouring libraries and free online courses to learn what she needed to know to work here. And she proved me wrong. These last two years, I thought I wanted her. But I've come to need her too, and I can't imagine not having her with me.

There's no way I can stand by while she dates other men.

"Ford, you okay?"

She's looking up at me wide-eyed and surprised. I don't usually zone out, but she's caught me. "Yeah, everything is good. So uh... Ollie has a soccer game today after school. I know he'd love for you to come."

She nods. "I'd like that. I mean, if I can talk my boss into letting me go a little early."

I roll my eyes and make my way back over to my seat. "Yeah, he's a real asshole, but I'm sure it will be okay."

She smirks and holds up her pad of paper. "Right, actually he's a pretty good guy. I still can't believe you paid for Carrie and Philips' honeymoon, Ford. It was too much, really. They wish you had been able to come to the wedding to thank you properly."

I grit my teeth because I had a business meeting in

the city and had to miss it. Fuck, it seems like I missed a lot. "No thanks are necessary, really. I was happy to do it."

I shrug because the money wasn't a big deal for me, but I wanted to give Carrie something that would make things easier for Lilian. And when she had talked about getting a second job to pay for a wedding gift, I knew I had to do something. It worked out, though, because it was about the time that my brother fired his assistant and Lilian started filling in for her too. I would have given her a raise even if she didn't help my brother out, but she was a lot easier to convince since she was taking on more of a workload. "Okay, so let's get to work. I have a birthday party to plan. Can you take some notes?"

She nods, and we both start brainstorming everything that needs to be done to pull off the best birthday party of the year. I normally try not to spoil my child, but after the last few months, he deserves to have a good time and be happy.

Now if I can just stay on the topic at hand. Because the whole time, I'm trying to figure out how I'm going to convince my assistant she should be dating me.

LILIAN

I pull into the parking lot of the community park. There are families everywhere, and it takes me back to years ago when Carrie played soccer. I get out of the car smiling as I spot my boss pulling into the lot. Waiting in front of my car, I try to steady my nerves and prepare myself. It's crazy because you would think after working for the man for two years, I wouldn't get butterflies in my stomach every time I'm around him, but I do. Of course, I don't think I'm the only woman affected by his thick hair that's flocked with silver or his blue piercing eyes and toned body. No, I'm just one of many.

"You made it," he says as he gets out of his black Mercedes.

I nod and gesture to my legs. "Yep, I even had time to run home and grab a pair of jeans."

We walk side by side toward the field. "So did Janet pick up Ollie from school?" I ask about the babysitter he hired a few months ago.

"Yep, she dropped him off anyway. She has a night class tonight."

I nod just as Ford sucks in a breath and mumbles darkly, "Fuck."

I look up at him in surprise. I've heard him curse before, plenty of times, but I'm not sure what would bring that reaction here of all places. "What's wrong?"

But before he can answer, one of the soccer moms I recognize from the other games I've been to waves at Ford. "Yoo-hoo, Ford! I'm glad you made it."

He grumbles and waves at her before turning us in the other direction to stand farther down the field. I can't help but laugh. "She's not giving up, is she?"

He shakes his head and looks over his shoulder. I swear the man looks stricken, which surprises me. Looking the way he does, he has to be used to women checking him out. "No, she's definitely not giving up. What about you? You going to help me out?"

My eyes flick up in surprise because the idea of helping him is definitely doable. I mean, half the time, I have to stop myself from reaching up and touching his hair, grabbing his hand, or kissing him. All things I shouldn't be thinking or doing as his assistant. But before I can ask him what he has in mind, the coach hollers for him.

He gives him the one-minute finger and says, "Shit."

I look around, expecting another mom to be heading our way, but when I don't find one, I ask him, "What's wrong now?"

He smiles at me and pushes a piece of hair off my face. I try not to gasp or let any emotions show. His thumb trails across my cheek, and then all of a sudden, it's gone. "I'm about to have a stern talking to."

I bite my lip. "By who?" I point to the coach. "Him?"

He nods. "Yep, I'm sure by now Ollie has told everyone about the party at the trampoline park, and Coach is not going to be happy—"

"We're not canceling. Ollie is going to be so excited, and we're not going to let him down." I say it before thinking and then, realizing it's not really my place, I tack on, "I mean, that's what I think anyway... I know you can do whatever you want."

He looks at me surprised but nods his head. "No, I agree with you. We're not canceling. I can handle a good talking to."

He walks away, and I know I shouldn't, but I watch him the whole time until he stops next to the coach. Ford had changed into jeans too, and even though he looks good in a nice pair of dress pants, the man can definitely fill out a pair of Levi's. Damn.

"Lily, Lily, you came."

I turn just in time as a sprinting Ollie leaps against me. I catch him as I fall down on my behind and wrap my arms around him with a laugh. "Of course, I came. I hear you're playing goalie today. I couldn't miss that."

"Did you hear I'm having a party? You'll come, won't you?"

Emotion hits me in the chest, and I don't try to examine it. "You want me at your birthday party?"

He rolls his eyes and gives me a big rolling, "Dddu-uuhhhh. Will you come?"

I nod. "I hear they have dodgeball there. You're going down, little Blaze!"

He cackles, stands up, flexes his little arms, and then points at me. "No, you're going down, Lily. Oh, it's on."

I get up and steady myself on my feet. "Oh, it's definitely on. I can't wait."

He turns and starts running toward his dad. They bump fists, and Ollie must be telling him about my challenge with dodgeball because Ford's head falls back with a laugh and he turns to look at me. Ollie runs to the field, and Ford is heading my way. He's still watching me, but now the smile is gone from his face. His gaze travels down my body and back up again. I can't take my eyes off him.

"Ford, hey, I'm so glad you came."

The woman comes out of nowhere and puts herself directly in the path of Ford. I hear him say, "Of course I came. My son's playing."

His tone is droll, and it's obvious that he's not happy about being stopped by the woman. I've heard the rumors, and the few times I've been to the games, I've seen it all in action. There are a few moms that seem determined to get their claws in him. I can't say I blame them, but I would expect a little more decorum from the women. I mean, there are kids all around.

She's not giving up, though. I see him step to the side, and then she does the same. I don't think about it, I just act. I walk toward them, slide around the woman, and position myself between her and Ford. I flatten my body to his and look up at his stunned face. My hands slide to his shoulders, and I go on my tiptoes as I pull him down to me. "Hey, honey. I'm sorry I was late."

His hands grip my hips as my lips meet his. I

should just give him a peck and pull back. We are at a soccer field that is filled with kids. But my thoughts are a jumble as his fingers dig into my denim-covered hips and he pulls me flush against him. The kiss deepens, and I slide my tongue against his. My nipples are pebbled, and I slide a little to the left just to feel them rub against his hard chest. My hands go around his neck, and I thread my fingers through the hair at his nape.

He groans, and that's what brings me to my senses. Not the people cheering because I guess the game has started. Not the coach hollering at the players to run and get the ball. Nope, I let him go when he groans into my mouth. If his eyes were wide before, they are hooded and about two shades darker now. He's watching me closely as I try to pull away.

He doesn't let me go far. I turn around, and the woman I interrupted is staring at us with her mouth hanging open. "Hi. I'm Lilian."

"Megan," she mutters before walking backwards. "I'm going to go watch the game from my seat."

I nod as I start to move, and Ford's hands grip my hips, holding me to him. "It was nice meeting you," I call to her.

I look at Ford over my shoulder. "Are we going to watch the game like this?"

He doesn't release his hold on my hips though. His cheeks are ruddy, and his hands tighten. "It's either that or everyone's going to see what I've got going on down there."

I gasp. Is he...? Does he mean? "Uhhhh, wait so, uh..." I stutter. I can't even form a sentence.

"Yeah. If you move, all the parents are going to see I'm hard. I mean, it's a normal reaction."

I squint in disbelief. "It's a normal reaction... to a kiss?"

He shrugs, taking a deep breath. "To your kiss... yeah, I guess so."

Speechless and feeling awkward, I shuffle my feet and accidentally rub against him. His grip tightens on me and holds me away from him a little. His groan is loud in my ear. "That's not helping."

I laugh up at him, and then it hits me. I just kissed my boss... and I liked it. By the bulge in his jeans, he liked it too. "So I should probably apologize. I thought I was helping the situation."

"You did. I think Megan got the picture."

He takes a deep breath, and I swear I hear him counting to ten. He eventually releases me and steps away. I turn to the ball game and watch. Neither Ford nor I say anything else about what just happened, which is good. I know I stepped over the line. Damn.

Is he going to fire me? I'm sure kissing your boss is against the rules or something.

I cheer for Ollie when he stops the ball from going into the net. I keep focused on the game until it's over and Ollie's team wins five to two.

Ollie is with his friends, celebrating their win, and I am looking everywhere but at Ford. "So I better go. Tell Ollie I'm proud of him. He did awesome."

He holds his hand out like he's going to touch me but then lets it drop suddenly. "I'm sure he's going to want to celebrate. Want to join us for dinner at Red's?"

I shake my head. "I can't. I'd love to, but I can't. I have a date."

"A date?" he asks. I swear he seems surprised. Is it really so unbelievable to think that a man wants to go out with me?

I nod and force a smile on my face. This is something my sister arranged. I swear she got married two days ago and she still had time to set me up. "Yep, a date. I know. Shocker, right?"

I start to walk away and wave at him over my shoulder. "I'll see you in the morning at work."

I turn before he can answer me. I try to get myself mentally prepared for my date, but the whole time all I can think about is that I wish I had gone to dinner with Ford and Ollie instead.

Ford

"Which book do you want to read tonight?" I ask Ollie as he jumps into his bed.

I'm standing at the bookshelf, looking at the rows of books but not seeing any of them. I can't seem to get that kiss with Lilian out of my head. We've never stood as close to each other as we did today. I've always respected that she was an employee and kept a professional distance. But after the way she fit her body to mine and that kiss, there's no way I'll be able to keep my distance now. That is if she doesn't fall in love with her date tonight. I suck in a breath to hold in my groan.

"Dad! Are you listening to me? I asked if Lilian could come and help me make my birthday cupcakes."

I grab a book off the shelf. We've read it at least ten times, so I know it's a favorite of his. I walk over to his bed and sit down on the end of it. "You do know that I can make cupcakes, right?"

He looks at me skeptically. "Really, Dad? Didn't Granny say you burned water?"

I laugh and grab on to his ankle under the cover. "Really? That was years and years ago. I'm a good cook now. Surely I can handle some cupcakes."

He sits up in bed. "So you've never made cupcakes before?"

I shrug. "Noooo, but how hard can it be? I'll read up on it."

He puts his hand on my arm. "Why can't we just ask Lilian? You know she'd do it."

I bite my lower lip. The truth is, when Granny was sick, I depended on Lilian to help with Ollie quite a bit. I made sure to give her time off at the office even though she never took it. I know Ollie has developed a bond with her, and a part of me should probably be worried about it. He's been hurt by his own mother. Do I want to risk hurting him again? No matter what, Ollie needs to be my priority. "You know what, Ollie? Lilian has her own life. She may be busy or have something else planned."

"Dadddd," he says, drawing my name out long and

loud. "Just ask her. I understand if she says no. But we should still ask her. She was pretty happy when I asked her to come to my party."

"You asked her to come to your party?"

"Duh, Dad! You told me to invite my friends. She's my friend."

My son is way smarter than I was at his age, that's for sure. "You're right. What was I thinking?"

He grabs the book from my hand. "Okay, I'm going to read. Why don't you go call Lilian and ask her?"

I look at the book that he already has opened on his lap. "You don't want me to read with you?"

He seems to think about it. "No, I can read it. I'd rather you call Lily."

I nod and stand up. "Got it. I'll go call her. You read for fifteen minutes and then I'll be back to tuck you in."

His little nose scrunches up. "Dad, I don't need to be tucked in. I'm six."

I get to the door and turn to face him. "You're still five until next week, so I'm tucking you in. I'll be back."

I shut his bedroom door and practically run down the steps.

I have been wondering all night how Lilian's date

went. The urge to call her earlier was almost unbearable. At least now I have an excuse to text.

I type out a message on my phone and stare at it.

> Hey. Ollie wanted me to ask you if you would come over and make cupcakes with him next week. He wants to take them to a school party, and he doesn't trust my baking skills.

I read it twice wondering if it's witty enough or if it makes me sound desperate.

I roll my eyes because I make multi-million dollar decisions on a regular basis, but what to say in a text has me second-guessing myself. I hit send before I can talk myself out of it.

The typing bubbles pop up, and I hold my breath, waiting for her reply to show on the screen.

> Sure. Is his school party next Friday? Should I come over the night before?

> That would be perfect. He'll be excited.

> Me too. Something to look forward to.

I stare at her response. I know it's none of my business, but I type out the one question I don't have the right to ask.

How was your date?

Her response is slower this time. So I type and hit send.

Are you still with him? Sorry for interrupting.

Her text pops up, and I let out a breath as I read.

No, I'm home. It was okay. He was nice and all but I won't be seeing him again.

I pump my fist into the air and am busy celebrating when my phone dings, letting me know I received another text.

Can we talk?

I suck in a breath. *Talk.* That sounds serious and could go either way for me, but I answer her yes before impatiently calling her.

As soon as she answers, I ask her, "Is everything

okay?"

"Yes, everything's fine."

"What did she say, Dad?" Ollie bellows down the stairs. I get up and walk to the landing so I can look up and see him. I tell Lilian to hold on a minute. "She said yes, she'd help you make cupcakes."

"Yes!" he says excitedly.

"I'm on the phone with her. I'll be up in a minute."

He nods. "Okay, Dad. Good night."

"Good night, bud," I tell him before getting back on the phone. "Sorry about that."

I can hear the smile on her face. "Was that excited scream because of me?"

I nod as I pace back and forth. "It was. He's really excited about the whole cupcake thing."

I swear it sounds like she claps her hands together. "Good. I'll have to bring my A game. I may even have to do a practice run before coming over. I haven't baked in a while. Carrie always wanted me to keep the sweets out of the house."

"Well, I appreciate you doing it... so what did you want to talk about?"

She blows out a breath, and the pause has me pulling the phone away to look at it to make sure we're still connected. "You there?"

Her voice softens. "Yeah, I'm here. I'm sorry. You're probably trying to get Ollie to bed. I can just talk to you about it tomorrow."

"No!" I practically shout into the phone, not wanting her to hang up. "I can talk now. What's up? What do you want to talk about?"

She sighs. "I just wanted to apologize for today...."

Her voice trails off, and I feel like I have been hit in the gut. "Apologize for what exactly?"

She laughs uncomfortably. "You're going to make me say it, aren't you? Okay, well, I know I sort of said so earlier, but I feel it's worth mentioning again. I'm sorry for the kiss. I really thought I was helping, but I shouldn't have pawed you at your son's soccer game."

"You didn't paw."

She laughs. "I beg to differ. I definitely didn't act professionally. Anyway, I wanted to apologize—again—and let you know that it wouldn't happen again. I don't want you to feel uncomfortable around me. I promise from this point forward, I'm keeping my hands—and my mouth—to myself."

My mouth falls open. It's on the tip of my tongue to tell her that she can kiss or touch me any time she wants, but obviously today made her uncomfortable. I don't want to pressure her and make her want to leave or quit. I clear my throat. "There's nothing you can do to make me uncomfortable. Don't worry about it. You and I are good, Lilian."

She lets out a breath of relief. "Really? I was worried you were going to fire me first thing in the morning."

"What?" I ask incredulously. "There's nothing you can do that would make me fire you. I can't make it without you. I know that."

Her voice goes all soft again. "Okay, good to know, boss."

When she calls me boss, it feels like she's putting us back on our professional footing. It's disappointing to me, but at least she's not quitting or anything. Because I wasn't lying to her; I couldn't make it without her.

"So I need to get Ollie into bed. I'll see you in the morning."

"Yeah, I'll see you in the morning. Please tell Ollie I'm excited about the cupcakes. Good night, Ford."

The sound of my name on her lips has me wishing she was here with me. "Night, Lilian."

I grip my phone in my hand and bang it into my other palm. Now that I've hung up, there's a thousand questions going through my head. The only calming thought I have is the fact that I'm going to see her in the morning.

LILIAN

When I walk into the office the next morning, I'm more tense than usual. I know that Ford said everything is okay, but I haven't been able to get that kiss off my mind. I no sooner get to my desk and Lucas, Ford's brother, comes to stand in front of me.

"I have someone coming in for an interview this morning. Hopefully we can get some help in here so you're not stretched so thin."

I shrug my shoulders. "Honestly, it's not bad at all. I'll help as long as you need me."

He laughs. "I'm glad you feel that way, but it's probably better if we get someone hired. I don't think my brother likes sharing you."

My eyes widen. I know what he meant by it, but after that kiss yesterday, my mind goes somewhere else. "Right. Well, I'll be happy to sit in and go over the details of the job with her."

"Good, good. Thanks, Lilian. Let me know when she gets here."

I nod and set my bag and purse down at my desk. I go about unpacking things. Every time I hear the elevator ding or a door open, I'm on edge wondering if Ford's coming and if it's going to be weird between us.

Once I have everything unpacked and put away, I barely get seated and a woman comes around the corner. "Hello. Can I help you?"

She smiles. "Yes, I'm Brandi Jones, and I'm here for an interview with Lucas Blaze."

I come around the desk. "Great. Hi, Brandi, I'm Lilian Steele. I'll be sitting in on the interview."

We shake hands, and I swear her smile drops a little. I try not to read anything into it and lean over my desk to intercom into Lucas' office. "Lucas, Ms. Jones is here for the interview."

"Great, I'll be right out."

I barely get the phone down before Lucas' office door opens and he comes striding down the hallway. I am about to introduce them when my phone rings, and I answer it. "Blaze Whiskey, this is Lilian."

"Lilian, hey, this is Isabella. Two things. We need to do lunch sometime soon, and I'm sorry to call your line, but Lucas left his phone on the counter here. Can I speak to him for a minute?"

"I would love to get together. We can schedule it after we get another assistant hired. And Lucas is standing right here. Hold on just a second."

I hold the phone in my hand and wait for Lucas and Ms. Jones to finish their introductions before interrupting. "Lucas, Issi's on the phone. Seems you left yours on the counter at home."

He laughs and takes the phone from me. "I did. Go on into the conference room, and I'll be right there."

I usher Ms. Jones down the hallway, but she keeps looking back at Lucas. Her voice is hushed while fanning herself with her hand. "Uh, well isn't he a hot one?"

I almost stumble on my feet before catching my bearings. *Did she really just say that?* "He's married. Happily married," I add.

She shrugs. "I can still look."

I get to the door of the conference room and hold the door open for her. She's not off to a good start, that's for sure. I point to a chair and sit down across from her. My tone with her has changed, but I know I need to keep an open mind. "Do you have your resume with you?"

She pulls it from the folder she's carrying and slides it across the table at me. "I do."

I scan her qualifications and previous jobs. "Tell me about your last job. What did you do there?"

She straightens in her seat. "Basic administrative tasks."

I wait for her to continue, and when she doesn't, I ask her, "Can you elaborate?"

She starts twirling her hair around her finger. "Well, typing. I made appointments. I worked closely with the boss."

"Do you know how many words you can type a minute?"

She lifts her shoulders as if she's unsure. "I don't know. Like twenty-five."

I look down at the resume to hide my surprise at the low number. "I'm assuming we can call your previous employer for a reference."

When she doesn't answer right away, I lift my head to look at her. She starts to nod and then quickly shakes her head side to side. "No, it's probably not a good idea. His wife works there too, and she wasn't very happy to find out he was having an affair."

Shocked, I look at her across the table, trying to read further into what she just said. "An affair?" I don't say anything else. I've learned that people want to talk about themselves, and in interviews you can't really ask all the questions you want to, but there's ways to getting answers just by listening.

She nods and juts her chin out. "Yes. I was sleeping with him, but that is over. He decided to stay with his wife."

Dumbfounded, I sit back in my seat. I don't even know where to go from here. Before I can say anything, the conference door opens, and instead of Lucas, who I'm expecting, it's Ford. He smiles when he spots me. "There you are." He tilts his head to the side with a worried look on his face. "You okay?"

I nod and glance across the table at Ms. Jones before looking at him. "Yes, yes, I'm fine. I'm helping Lucas with an interview. Ms. Jones, this is Ford Blaze. He's the CEO of Blaze Whiskey."

She stands up and practically glides around the table to him. She shakes his hand by wrapping both hers around it. Ford takes it all in stride, though. I think he's used to being hit on by women. I barely resist rolling my eyes. "Do you need me for something?" I ask Ford.

He pulls his hand from Ms. Jones' and turns away from her. "Yeah. When you're done, can you stop in my office?"

I nod. "Sure, this shouldn't take long."

He nods, waving over his shoulder as Ms. Jones gushes goodbye to him. As soon as the door closes behind him, she's turning on me. "My God! How do you get any work done around here? I'd be too busy looking at the décor."

"Décor?" I stutter.

She nods emphatically. "What else would you call it? Lucas is hot, but Ford is Daddy Hot."

I feel as if my eyes pop out of my head. "Excuse me? Daddy hot?"

Ms. Jones shrugs her shoulders. "Come on, that silver head of hair, deep voice, strong jawline, and those lips." She starts to fan herself. "He is H-O-T."

As soon as she sits back down in her chair, Lucas comes in. "Sorry to keep you waiting, ladies. Now—"

I hold Ms. Jones' resume in my hands and cut Lucas off. "It's okay. The interview is over. Ms. Jones, unfortunately, I don't think you'll be a good fit for the company. Thank you for coming in. I'll be happy to show you out."

Her mouth drops, and when she closes it, she's

glaring at me. "Mr. Blaze was supposed to interview me, not you."

Lucas is taken back by my attitude and seems shocked as he looks between me and the other woman. I hold up her resume. "It says here that you worked at Jasper Mountain Coaster from 2020 through 2022. It didn't open until the end of 2021. You admitted to only typing twenty-five words a minute, and the job description requires more. When I asked about your previous work, you admitted to doing a little typing, scheduling, and having an affair with your boss. You said that you didn't know how you'd get any work done with all the hot men in the building. Now, while here, you've talked inappropriately about Lucas and then called Ford 'Daddy Hot.' Unfortunately, I believe you are a lawsuit waiting to happen, and like I said, not a good fit." I turn to Lucas. "Of course, if you would like to interview her—"

He cuts me off, holding both his hands up. "Nope, it sounds like you got it." He turns to Ms. Jones. "Thank you for coming in, but the interview is over. I'll see you out."

I know I should let him do it, but I stand up and hold the door open. "No, really. I'll be happy to see Ms. Jones out the door."

Lucas almost looks worried. I don't know if he thinks I'm going to start a fight or what, but he doesn't argue with me about it. Ms. Jones huffs loudly and stands up. She glares at me as she walks past, and I follow behind her, making sure she makes it all the way to the exit. When I mutter "good riddance" as the door closes behind her, I turn and run almost directly into Lucas.

He's rubbing his hand across his chin. "Thank you for handling that, Lilian."

I cross my arms over my chest. "Sorry if I overstepped—"

He laughs and shakes his head. "You didn't overstep. My brothers and I appreciate everything you do here. I know you have the company's best interests at heart."

I nod. "Okay, uh, Ford asked to see me when we were done. Do you need anything from me today?"

He waves his hand in front of himself. "No, you have everything caught up. I'm good."

He shoves his hands in his pockets. "Issi's going to drop my phone off. I'm going to meet her outside if any of my brothers are looking for me."

I start walking toward my desk. "Tell Issi I said hi."

He hollers he will as he walks out the door.

I grab a pad of paper and a pen off my desk before

making my way to Ford's office. The whole way, I'm trying to convince myself that I did the right thing. I ended the interview because she was inappropriate. It didn't have anything to do with the fact that she was lusting after Ford. I was not jealous.

FORD

"How did the interview go?" I ask Lilian when she knocks on my open door. I was actually happy to learn that someone had come in for an interview, but when I walked in earlier, it didn't seem like it was going well.

She purses her lips. "She wasn't a good fit."

I don't question her reasoning. Lilian is usually a good judge of people.

"I'm sorry to hear that. I know it's hard on you doing the work of two people."

She sits down in the chair and fidgets with the pen in her hand. "It's really not that bad.

I'd rather take the time to hire someone that is going to do a good job and mesh well with everyone than just hire someone because we need to fill the spot."

I hold my hands up because she almost seems defensive about it. "Hey, I'm not complaining. I'm just asking if it gets to be too much for you, to let me know. I don't want you to be unhappy here."

She blinks her long lashes at me. "Okay, thank you. I appreciate it, but I promise, I'm fine."

"Okay, so catch me up on meetings for this week."

She pulls out her phone where my calendar is synced. She's tried repeatedly to show me how to do it all on my own phone, but I like having her come in here every week so we can talk and go over things.

She starts to scroll on her phone and relays the various meetings I have. The whole time she talks, I'm taking her in, watching the way she pushes her hair behind her ear, the way she pauses and bites her lower lip. When she lifts her eyes to mine, they widen, and she looks back at me.

In a daze, I clear my throat. I have no idea what all she just said, but thankfully, I can look at my computer and hopefully figure it out. She'll make sure I don't miss anything anyway.

"Thank you again for coming to the game last night. It meant a lot to Ollie. He was excited to finally get to try his hand at goalie."

She rolls her eyes "It's about time he got to play that position. Is the coach blind? He has to realize that his son is not the best choice for that. I know he keeps putting him there, but he needs to put him in a position where... well, let's just say. You can't hide as goalie, is all I'm saying. Ollie rocked it last night."

I chuckle. "You seem to feel really strongly about it."

She throws a hand up. "I don't like that Ollie is being messed with, that's all. I just need five minutes with the coach, and I'm pretty sure we could be seeing eye to eye on things."

I choke back the emotion that hits me. His own mother doesn't even care to call and check on him, and here this woman is, ready to go to war for him.

"All right there, killer. We don't need to be planning a rebellion or anything. I told Ollie he just needs to keep working, and if he works hard enough, there's no way he can't play him. It will work out."

She rolls her eyes. "I like my way better."

I get up and move toward her, leaning against my desk. "I feel like your way may end up with someone in jail."

She lifts her shoulders and shrugs like facing jail time would be worth it or something.

I lift my chin at her. "All right, so how's your schedule for this week? Anything going on?"

I try to be nonchalant about it, but I'm sure it's obvious that I'm trying to find out if she's going on any more dates.

She leans back in her chair. "I have a meeting with the new office supply store in Jasper. I think we can get paper and toner cheaper than what we're paying right now. I also plan to post some more ads for help. I know we can find better applicants than Ms. Jones."

I cross my arms over my chest and try to appear relaxed. I normally try to refrain from asking anything personal, but besides being worried about her with Carrie married now, I'm also wondering if she has any more dates planned. "So how's it going with Carrie? You doing okay at the house by yourself?"

"Carrie is loving her honeymoon. She and Philip are having a blast, and well, I haven't really had time to notice Carrie being gone. She's made it so that I stay busy while she's away."

"Oh yeah?" I ask as my stomach drops. I have a feeling I know what she's about to say.

She rolls her eyes. "Yeah, uh, I have another date tonight."

I pop off the edge of my desk and walk around to sit down in my chair. I'm trying to act like I'm not bothered, but my jaw tightens. "I thought you weren't going out with that guy again."

Her face turns red. "Uh, yeah, this is a different guy. I really think that Carrie was worried about me, and she set me up with some dates while she was gone. Either that, or she thought I couldn't get one on my own. But yeah, we're going dancing at the Whistler tonight."

Gritting my teeth, I ask her, "Someone you know?"

She nods. "Well, I met him at the wedding. He works with Philip."

I'm on the verge of asking her not to go—that she needs to date me and no one else when my office door opens and Lucas looks in. He's rolling his eyes as he looks at me. "Did she tell you about the interviewee?"

Lilian looks guilty and turns in her seat to answer Lucas. "Uh, yeah, I told him she wasn't a good fit."

Lucas laughs. "That's it? Good, because we don't need for his head to get even bigger."

I look between the two of them. "What's that supposed to mean?"

Lucas chuckles and then does air quotes. "Ms. Jones thinks you're Daddy Hot." He shrugs his shoulders and gestures to me. "I guess some people are into the premature gray. I don't see it, but whatever. No worries, Lilian took care of it. She ended the interview before I could say a word and escorted the woman out of the building."

Lilian's face just keeps getting redder, and she's looking at me defiantly. "She wouldn't have been a good fit here."

Lucas agrees. "Yeah, I'm glad you took care of it, but we really need to give you another raise or bonus if we don't hire someone soon."

Lilian stands and makes her way to the door. "I'm good, really. You guys need to quit worrying about me. Do you need anything else from me, Ford? I'll be at my desk if so."

She hightails it out of my office, and before Lucas can escape, I ask him, "Hey, you and Issi want to go out tonight?"

He leans on the chair that Lilian just vacated. "Uh, you want to go out? Who are you and what did you do with my brother?"

"Har, har, little brother. I DO have a life, you know. You want to go or not?"

"I think we are going to sit this one out. Friday is when I leave for the Vegas conference, and Issi can't go with me, so I think we're going to hang at home tonight. You have someone to watch Ollie?"

I wince when I realize that I didn't even think

about having someone to watch Ollie. On the rare occasion I do go out, it was always Granny that watched him. I hired a part-time babysitter, but I haven't asked her to ever watch him so I can go out. It's been more for after-school care and rides to practice and games. "Uh, no but—"

Before I can finish, my brother holds his hand up. "We'll watch him."

"Are you sure? Maybe you should ask Issi first."

He laughs. "Have you met my wife? She loves having Ollie over." He pulls out his phone and starts to text while he's talking. "I'm texting her now, but I promise she's going to love it. She'll make some kind of plans to entertain-" He cuts off when his phone dings and then holds it up. "See, she says awesome. She's going to make his favorite homemade pizza and the series they started watching the last time he was over has a new installment. So we got Ollie. I'll pick him up at your house around five?"

I nod. "Thanks man, I appreciate it. I'll have him ready."

He nods and starts to walk out the door before turning back to me. "Wait. Where you going tonight?"

"The Whistler," I tell him, naming the only bar in Whiskey Run.

He rears back in surprise. "You're using a kid free

night to go to the Whistler? All right, what's going on?"

"Nothing's going on."

He doesn't believe me, though. "Bullshit, bro. What's up?"

I shrug and do my best to act as if my request is completely normal when we both know it's not. "Nothing. Lilian mentioned that she was going on a date there tonight, and I thought... I don't know what I thought really."

His mouth falls open, and then he starts to stutter. "But, but..." He shuts my office door and walks over, falling into the seat that Lilian just left a few moments ago. "Ford. No, you can't do this. We need Lilian. You can't mess with what we have going on here."

I refuse to rise to the bait even though it's pissing me off. "I seem to remember having almost the exact conversation with you about your wife. Look how that turned out."

"Yeah, but Lilian works here. You're her boss. If it goes south—and let's face it; you don't have the best track record—if it goes south, we're both out of an assistant. We need her."

I slam my fist onto my desk and lean over it, chest heaving. "I need her, dammit. It has nothing to do with her job here or anything else. I need her. For the last two years, she's consumed my every thought, but I stayed away because she wasn't dating... she wasn't ready for a relationship."

"What... now she is?"

I shrug and start to pace back and forth across my office. "I don't know. Fuck, I don't know, Lucas. But I do know that I can't just stand by and not find out."

"Shit. Fine. I got Ollie. I wish Huddy was in town. Take Beau with you tonight, not Austin."

I don't question him. Huddy is our brother that is serving overseas somewhere. I'm sure he wants me to take Beau because he thinks Beau can keep me in line and Austin is the type to instigate things. "Fine."

Lucas gets up and goes to the door. "I'm telling you, Ford. You better be right about this. I don't want to lose her here just because you can't keep it in your pants."

I don't try to hide my feelings. I can't anymore. "It's more than that, bro. I promise."

He nods in understanding, and I think he gets it. He's softened since he and Isabella got married. Before he gets out the door, he grunts at me, "Don't fuck it up."

"I won't," I mutter to the empty room. The truth is, fucking this up is not an option.

I send a text to Austin and Beau.

Lucas and Issi are watching Ollie tonight. Either of you up for going to the Whistler and having a few beers with me?

Beau's reply is immediate.

Can't. Sorry bro.

As I'm looking at my phone, I get a reply from Austin.

I'm in. Meet you there at six.

I thumbs-up his message and send a middle finger emoji to Beau. Invigorated now, I need a plan. Lilian is going to be mine. She just doesn't know it yet.

Lilian

I may need to rethink things.

Maybe with all the changes recently, I shouldn't be making rash decisions.

I look across the table at my date. Not that dating is a rash decision. I mean, the guy seems nice enough. But is this what I want?

My thoughts go to Ford, and I know they shouldn't. I shouldn't be thinking of my hot older boss. I shouldn't be thinking about that kiss we shared, and I sure shouldn't be wondering what he's doing right now.

I take a sip of water, and it turns into a gulp. As if drinking the water is going to wash my thoughts away. If only it was that easy.

Come on, Lilian. Put in some effort here.

I clear my throat and put the water down. "So tell me about you, Ty."

He doesn't answer. Instead, he points at my drink. "Are you sure you're good with water? I can get you another drink or something. Maybe some of that Blaze Whiskey."

I laugh at his joke. You'd think since I work at one of the largest whiskey distilleries in Tennessee, I'd drink the stuff. And I do... sometimes. But I'm thinking for a first date, water is a better idea.

"Thank you, Ty. Water is good. Especially when we get back out there," I tell him, pointing to the dance floor.

"You sure do like to dance."

I nod enthusiastically even though dancing is really not my favorite thing. But I do prefer it to sitting here trying to figure out what to say to the man in front of me when I'm thinking about Ford.

"So you work with Philip. Are you in sales like him?"

He nods and finishes off his drink. "I am. At least for now, anyway. If Philip takes the promotion, then he'll be moving on and up."

I'm focused now. "Promotion?"

He nods. "Yeah, the company offered him a promotion to regional sales director. He's supposed to give an answer when he gets back from his honeymoon." His eyes get big. "Do you know what his answer's going to be?"

I shake my head. "No, I don't have a clue."

My mind starts to whirl. Carrie hasn't said anything to me about it. I have a thousand questions, like what exactly does this promotion entail, but I'm not going to ask. I'll wait to hear from Carrie. I push my glass away. "You ready to get back out there?"

He laughs. "Yeah, let's go work up an appetite."

I nod and lead the way to the dance floor. It's a line dance, and for the next few minutes, Ty and I laugh over our missteps. It's when I feel a tingle at my neck that I look up and stumble on my feet. Ford and Austin are sitting at a table a few feet away. Austin is talking, but Ford's eyes are on me.

What's he doing here? I don't think he normally hangs out here after work through the week. I'm pretty sure he spends most of his time at Ollie's sporting events or at home.

Ty takes my brief stumble as meaning we need to take a break. "Come on, let's go order some food. I'm starving."

I point toward Ford and Austin and tell Ty I'm
going to go say hi. I'm not sure if he hears me, but he
follows behind me. Ford watches me the whole way to
him, if he notices Ty, he doesn't act like it. As soon as I
stop next to the table, I ask, "Where's Ollie?"

"He's with Lucas and Isabella."

I nod. "So what are you two doing here?" I want to
ask him if he remembers me saying I had a date here
tonight. Did he come here because of me? I've noticed
a difference between the two of us, and I'm not sure
what to think.

Austin's head is swinging between Ford and me,
but he's not saying a word, which is weird for him.
Ford's eyes never leave mine. "I wanted to come and
check things out."

"Oh!" I say.

After a brief silence, Austin leans forward. "Hey.
I'm Austin, and this is my brother, Ford. We work
with Lilian."

"She's mine... I mean, she's my assistant." Ford says
with a glaring smile at Ty.

I merely stand here, tongue-tied when I feel Ty
press to my back as he leans forward to shake hands
with them. I cough and move away from Ty's touch,
my eyes still on Ford. I swear I see disapproval in his

face before I force my gaze away. "Guys, this is Ty. He works with my sister's husband."

Ford shakes Ty's hand, and I watch as Ford's forearm flexes and his jaw tightens. When Ty pulls his hand away, he flexes it and shakes it before dropping it to his side. I put a hand on his shoulder. "So we should probably go and eat. I'm starving. You hungry, Ty?" I don't wait for him to answer before I start pushing him away from the table. "Bye, guys, see you in the morning," I tell Ford and Austin before making it across the room to our table.

As soon as I sit down in my seat, I realize that when I look at Ty, Ford is in my vision right over his shoulder. I try to ignore the glare from Ford, but it's impossible because I swear i can feel his eyes on me.

Ty waves down the waitress, and she comes over with her pad and pencil. "What can I get you?"

She's looking at Ty, smiling, but he gestures to me. "I'll take the chicken sandwich and French fries."

Ty puts the menu back in the holder at the middle of the table. "I'll take the same."

"Sure thing," she says before walking off.

I turn in my seat, but no matter what I do, if I look at Ty, my eyes are drawn to Ford across the room. It's not helping matters that his eyes are still glued on me.

I'm trying not to be obvious, but Ty waves his hand in front of my face. "Lilian, everything okay?"

I nod with a jerk of my head. "Yes, yes, sorry. What were you saying?"

He leans across the table, and instinctively I lean back. "So your boss... he's pretty intense."

I shrug and am saved when the waitress comes back with refills. I pick up the glass. "You think so? I've never noticed that."

I take a drink of water as Ty continues. "Yeah, he seems protective of you. Like an older brother or something."

I start to choke on the water, and I set the glass down with a bang. "Older brother?" I squeak.

He pats me on the back. "You okay?"

I nod, and he shrugs. "Yeah, exactly like an older brother. I mean, he's too old for—"

I cut him off. "He's forty-five. He's not old."

He seems taken back at my defensive tone. "Yeah, but you're what... thirty... uh in your twenties?"

I tsk him. "Women don't like to talk about their age, Ty." It never bothers me. Any other time, I'd tell him I was thirty years old and not think anything about it, but not if he's going to insinuate Ford is too old for me.

I let my gaze travel across the room again, and

Ford's watching me with a tense look on his face. He looks worried, and I know exactly what he's asking me by the look on his face. He's wondering if I'm okay. Damn, could Ty be right? Does Ford think of me like a little sister? Did he come here tonight just to make sure I'm okay? I suck in a breath and force a smile to my face, letting him know I'm okay.

At that moment, Ty looks over his shoulder. Ford doesn't even seem upset to be caught staring at me. Ty turns to me. "So it's like that, is it?"

My face heats. "Like what?"

He points at me. "You and your boss?"

I don't even know what to say. I can't tell him that I kissed my boss the other day and haven't stopped thinking about him ever since.

Ty leans closer with a smile on his face. He doesn't look mad. "So... you and your boss?"

I shake my head. "No, we aren't together, if that's what you're asking."

He laughs. "I'm thinking he may feel differently."

"Ty—" I start, but he cuts me off by holding his hands up. "It's okay. Hey, this is a first date. I didn't expect your boss to be here, obviously staking his claim—"

I shake my head. "It's not like that."

He laughs. "I think it is, and I think if you were

honest with yourself, you may be feeling the same way."

He gets up from the table, and I reach for him. "Don't leave, please. At least eat your dinner."

He runs his hands down his shirt. "Oh, I'm not leaving. I have a feeling this is going to get good. I'm running to the men's room. I'll be right back."

He walks away, and as soon as he's gone, our food is being delivered.

Our waitress stops next to the table and looks unsure. "Lilian, right?"

I nod, surprised. I've only been in here a few times, and that was when Isabella had me come here to sing karaoke. "I'm sorry. I'm horrible with names. You're...?"

She nods nervously. "Tina. I'm Tina and this is so awkward, but I have to ask... uh, I'm wondering... oh gosh, I'm just wondering if you and Ty are together... like a couple?"

I shake my head and scrunch my nose up. "No, this is our first date, and I think we just agreed to be friends." I laugh as I realize how true my words are. Dating is not panning out like Carrie had hoped. "Why? Are you interested in Ty?"

She blushes, holding the tray against her chest.

"I've noticed him a few times he's been in here, but I'd never talk to him if he's with someone."

"Well, we're not together, so don't feel bad about talking to him. Maybe even give him your number."

She gasps. "I couldn't do that, no way."

The curvy waitress is beautiful, but she obviously doesn't know it. "I can feel things out for you."

Her eyes about pop out of her head. "You would do that?"

"Absolutely. Here he comes."

She immediately puts her head down and starts walking away. I'm bouncing in my seat as Ty gets back to the table. I feel like I've sort of ruined things tonight, and at least one of us should have a good time.

"What are you smiling about?" he asks as he sits down.

I take a bite of my sandwich and chew slowly. When I swallow, I take a drink of water. "So we agree that this is not going to go anywhere, right?"

He pops a French fry in his mouth. "Right. I try not to date women that are into other men."

"Har. Har. I'm not dating my boss—" He starts to talk, but I stop him. "Anyway, I have good news. While you were in the bathroom, the waitress asked about you."

He turns in his seat looking around, but Tina is

nowhere to be found. When he turns back to face me, I see her pop up from behind the bar, and I can't help but laugh.

He points between the two of us. "Our waitress?"

I nod. "Yep, the pretty blonde."

"She is pretty." He grimaces. 'Sorry, I'm sure I'm not supposed to say a woman is pretty when I'm on a date."

I take another bite of my sandwich and barely swallow it before I start talking. "Nope, we're friends. We've already agreed this is just two friends, hanging out. I think you and Tina should talk. You should get her number."

He seems to think about it and shakes his head. "I can't get a girl's number when I'm on a date with a woman. That's not right."

Man, he is a good guy. I hold my hands out and shake them. "We're friends. This is no longer a date. This is two friends hanging out. Think of me as your wingman—or wingwoman. We're going to get you her digits before this night is over with."

He crosses his arms and leans on the table. "I don't know. Are you sure about this? Are you setting me up? Is this a test or something?"

I hold my hands up. "This is not a test. We're friends, and I want to help a friend out. This is happening, Ty. We're going to get you a date out of this."

He shrugs his shoulders and starts eating again. I force my eyes to my plate because I know if I look across the room, I'm going to be looking into Ford's tempting blue eyes, wondering if maybe—just maybe —he does feel something more for me.

FORD

"Is there a reason that we're here spying on your assistant?"

I drag my gaze off Lilian and her date. "I'm not spying on Lilian."

Austin is smiling at me as he brings the glass to his lips. He sips on the whiskey and smirks. "Okay, so you haven't been watching her since we got here?"

I shrug. "She doesn't know that guy. I'm just making sure she's okay, that's all."

"Hello!" Austin holds his hand out to me like he wants to shake hands or something. "Hi. I'm Austin Blaze, your brother. I've known you literally my whole life, and if you're not into Lilian then I'll sign over my portion of Blaze Whiskey to the next person that comes in the door."

I try to hold in my smirk, but it's impossible to do around Austin. "Yeah, okay. Fine. If you're going to tell me it's a bad idea or I'm too old for her or something else asinine, then you can shut the fuck up."

He chuckles. "Fuck, dude, you're all tore up, aren't you? Why would I do any of those things? I think it's a great idea."

Surprised, I look at him. "You do?"

He slaps me on the shoulder. "Hell yeah, man. She's great with Ollie. He loves her. She makes you happy. Before she came to the company two years ago, no one could stand to be around you."

I cut him off. "I had divorced a cheating ex and was raising a three-year-old on my own, so yeah, sorry if I wasn't Mr. Congeniality."

He shrugs. "You're forgiven. I mean, you're a little old for her, but I think she's into it. And obviously she's changed her rule of not dating."

I start to nod and then ask, "How did you know about her rule?"

He shrugs, takes a drink of his whiskey, and sets the glass down. "I asked her out."

My whole body tenses, and I can feel the vein in my neck vibrating. "You asked her out? You asked my Lilian out?"

He looks at my hands forming fists on the table

between us and holds his hands up. "Uh, I didn't know she was YOUR Lilian, first of all. But don't worry, I do now. The point is, she said no."

"Stay the fuck away from her," I warn him.

He rolls his eyes and shrugs. "I do a lot of shit, but I don't mess with my brothers' women. I think I learned that lesson when I stole Lucas' girlfriend in 9th grade."

"Don't look at her either," I warn him.

He barks a laugh at that. "*Don't look at her*. Do you hear yourself? Geez, bro, you're all worried about me, and obviously you don't need to be. She told me no. But she's here... with that guy."

He turns in his seat and looks across the room. Lilian is smiling between the waitress and her date. "The question is, what are you going to do about him?"

That's all I've thought about. She says she's dating and she wants to have fun. "She says she's not looking for anything serious."

Austin gives me a strange look. "For the right guy, she would be."

"What do you know about it?"

He shrugs. "I'm just saying that she can say she just wants to have fun, but for the right guy, it could be more."

"Where's Ally? I haven't seen her in a while." I ask him about the girl that's been his best friend for what seems like forever.

"Probably at home. Anyway, we're not here to talk about Ally or me, for that matter. We need to talk about your woman on a date with another man."

"Fuck!" I mutter as I slam my fist on the table. I'm usually in control, and right now, I don't feel like I'm in control of anything.

"I don't know what to—fuck, she's coming this way."

I sit straighter in my seat as Lilian stops next to our table. "I'm heading home, but I thought I'd say good night."

"How was your date?" I blurt.

Austin coughs, and I swear I hear him say, "Smooth, bro."

She looks at her date, who is now sitting with the waitress. "We decided to be friends, and I fixed him up with the waitress."

My mouth drops open. I wasn't expecting that, but things are looking up... until I really think about it. "Wait. Did he disrespect you? Did he really hook up with someone else when he's on a date with you?"

I get up from my seat, ready to go wipe the floor with his punk ass when she stops me. Her hand wraps around my forearm. "No, it wasn't like that. I wanted... we're just friends, it's good. I promise."

Towering over her, I put a hand on her shoulder. "Do you need a ride home?"

She pulls her phone from her pocket. "No, I'm going to get an Uber."

"No, you're not. Austin, I'm heading out. You good?"

He's smiling ear to ear. "I'm good. See you two at work tomorrow."

I throw a hundred dollar bill on the table and then put my hand on the small of Lilian's back. "Let's go."

We get outside, and as we're walking to my car, she says, "You know I could've found my own ride home, right?"

"Why would you? I can take you home. I'm happy to."

I hit the unlock button on my car and open the passenger car door for her. She slides in easily, and I take my time, making my way to the driver's seat. I take a few calming breaths. "Are you really okay with all this?"

"With Ty?"

I nod and pull out onto the road. "Yeah, with Ty."

She nods, folding her hands together in her lap. "I'm more than okay with it."

I grip the steering wheel, and we ride in comfortable silence toward her house. I want to ask her if she's over this whole dating thing and exactly what she's looking for, but I'm afraid of the answer. I think about the fact that she's dating now and obviously looking for something. I know I need to take things slowly so I don't fuck it up. Obviously, Lucas will be pissed if I do.

An idea forms in my head, and before I can talk myself out of it, I ask her, "What are you doing this weekend?"

"Uummm—"

I interrupt her before she tells me that she has another date. "Go to Vegas with me. Lucas was dreading this trip and leaving Isabella. I thought I'd go in his place and take you with me."

She turns sideways in her seat. "You want me to go to Vegas with you?"

I shrug. "Yeah, it would be good. You said yourself that you want to travel. Have you been to Vegas before?"

"I've never been out of Tennessee."

"See! It would be great. We can get some work done. Do a little sightseeing."

At a stop sign, I look over at her. It takes everything in me not to insist that she goes with me, but in the end, I know the decision is up to her.

She withdraws into herself the rest of the way to her house, and I figure that she's going to say no. I want to convince her, but I also know that pressuring her is not the right thing to do. I can't make her spend time with me, even though that's exactly what I want to do. I'm tiptoeing around this because I don't want to fuck this up and lose her at the office.

When I pull into her driveway, I park and run around to her side to open the car door for her. I walk her up the walkway and stop at her front door. She looks at me and worriedly bites her lower lip. I want to reach up and run my thumb across it, but instead I put my hands in my pockets. Obviously, my request has stressed her out. "I'm not ordering you to go, Lilian. It was just a thought."

She leans her head back to look up at me. "Are you asking me because you want me to go or are you asking me to go because you feel sorry for me?"

"Feel sorry for you? What are you talking about? I'm asking you because I want you to go with me."

She finally tells me what I want to hear. "Okay, I'll go with you to the conference. Thank you for asking me."

I nod to her front door. "Go on in. I'll see you in the morning."

She unlocks her door and walks inside. She opens her mouth, closes it, and then opens it again. "Thanks for the ride home, Ford. I'll see you in the morning."

I nod, and she shuts the door. I barely make it to my car and I'm pulling my phone out. I call Lucas, and he answers on the second ring. "Hello."

"Hey, how's my son?"

"He just went to sleep. How was tonight?"

"Good. Hey, how would you like to skip Vegas?"

Lucas sighs. "You know I can't. Besides the conference, I'm having dinner with Jim Ogle while I'm there. He's an ass, but he does a lot of business with us. I can't cancel now."

I flip my phone over to the speakers in the car. "What if you don't cancel, but I go in your place?"

He pauses. "Wait. You're willing to go to Vegas... to a conference... so I can stay here?"

"Yeah, if you can watch Ollie."

"You know we'll watch Ollie."

I let out an excited breath. I might as well tell him; he's going to find out sooner or later. "And I'm taking Lilian."

He laughs. "I thought you were trying to help me out. Hell, you're just trying to get you—"

I interrupt him. "Don't you dare finish that sentence."

"A date. I was going to say date, that's all. Shit, Ford. Are you sure about this?"

I'm smiling ear to ear. I feel more lighthearted than I have in a long time. "I've never been so sure about anything in my life."

He groans. "I have a feeling I'm going to regret this but sure, yeah, I'd like to stay here. We'll have to go over things before you leave, and I'll give you a list of people to make sure you introduce yourself to while you're there, but sure, if you're up for it, I'm game."

"I owe you, brother."

He snorts. "I'm not so sure about that. I get to stay at home with my wife. You're going to Vegas to work. We'll just call it even."

"Sounds good."

We talk a little more, and I'm hanging up as I pull into my garage. I barely get into the door and my phone dings. I see the group text I have with my brothers pop up. Austin's message reads,

> Ford took me to spy on his
> assistant on a date. He's got it bad
> for Lilian. You guys should have
> seen him. He's whipped.

The first response is Beau.

> You're the CEO, Ford. You know better.

Lucas is next.

> I already gave him hell about it earlier today. There's no changing his mind.

And then Austin. He may have thrown me under the bus with that text, but he's the first to come to my defense.

> This is a good thing guys. Fuck. Let the man live a little.

There's no response from Huddy. We include him on the group text even though he never responds. Usually because he's stationed somewhere with no service. Usually once a month, we get some random text from him, letting us know he's alive.

I like the message from Austin and then send them all a middle finger emoji before shutting off my phone. Nothing is going to bring me down tonight.

LILIAN

I worked hard the next few days to get everything caught up since I'd be out of the office most of the day on Friday. I feel like I don't let out a breath until I'm seated on the Blaze brothers' private jet and Ford and I are on our way to Vegas.

The crew is preparing for takeoff, and Ford and I have not said much since we've sat down. "Having second thoughts?" he asks.

I shake my head. "No, I'm excited to go."

He turns in his seat and leans forward. "Something's bothering you. Spill it."

I've never talked about my private life at work. I've definitely never had any heartfelt conversations with my boss either. But I need to talk to someone. I have to get this off my chest, and it's only right he knows. "It's Carrie."

"Is she okay?" he asks, concerned.

I wave it off. "She's fine. They are due to get back from their honeymoon this weekend, and she's fine. But she called and talked to me last night and…"

I let my voice trail off because I'm not sure how to say it.

He reaches across the arm rest and puts his hand on my wrist. "Tell me. You can talk to me."

I let out a sigh and lean back, closing my eyes. "Gosh, I haven't talked about it in a long time, but after our parents passed away and it was just Carrie and me… she had extreme nightmares."

His voice is deep and thoughtful. "I can imagine it was hard for both of you."

I peek at him through my lashes, and his eyes are filled with concern. I turn my head to look at him fully now. "Yeah, it was, but maybe harder for her. She was eleven. After that, she would have panic attacks if I left her alone. She couldn't go to school for weeks, she was in therapy trying to learn how to deal with it all, and it helped, but she still had these feelings that something bad was going to happen… to me. That I would leave her. I could barely leave her side. I had to hire someone to sit with her so I could work at the diner at night when she was asleep just so I could make money. It was a mess for a long time, but she got better. A lot better..."

"But?"

I smile sadly. "No, no but. She did get better. She started to excel, she really started to do better after high school and when she met Philip. She still has panic attacks, but he can usually help her through them. He's really understanding and helpful."

He nods. "That's good. That has to be a relief for you."

I nod. "It is. But she called me last night and told me about a job offer Philip was given. His company wants to promote him, and it's more money. It would be out of state, but he doesn't feel like he should turn it down, not with them just starting out."

Ford is quiet, searching my face, and I see the second he reaches a conclusion. His voice is husky. "And if they go, she thinks you should go too?"

I reach over and put my hand on his arm. "That's what she said, but I don't know. We're going to talk about it when she gets home. Maybe I can go for a few weeks and help her get settled and then come home. I know she's an adult, but I will always think of her as that little girl that would cling to me. She's my little sister but—"

He wraps his hand around mine. "But she's like your daughter. I get it. I understand. Whatever you need to do, we'll make it work."

I look at him with eyes wide. "You need an assistant... I can't expect you to just hold my job for me. Not when everything is so in the air."

He laces our fingers together. "We'll make it work. I completely understand your need to be there for Carrie. I would do the same for Ollie. But I want you to know, I'm not just going to let you go, Lilian. I need you."

It's on the tip of my tongue to ask him what he means. Does he need me as his assistant or something more? Quickly I push that thought away. One kiss and I can't seem to get him out of my head. "Well, nothing is set in stone, and I'm going to talk to her and Philip when we get back."

The pilot comes to stand in front of us. "Ford, we're ready for takeoff."

He nods. "Sounds good, Ben. Thanks."

He looks at me curiously before turning away and walking toward the front of the plane.

"What does Philip do?"

"He does sales. He went to school for marketing, and he's like a top salesman at the big dealership in Jasper. He's really good, too, from what I hear. I met his boss at the wedding, and he raved on and on about him."

Ford nods, and he's about to pull his hand away when the plane starts to move. I squeeze it and then force myself to let go and squeeze the armrest instead. Ford looks at my white knuckles. "Shit, Lilian. You've never flown before?"

I shake my head stiffly. "Nope. I'm fine. We're fine. No big deal."

I can feel his eyes on me, and I concentrate on taking deep breaths and letting them out slowly.

He pries my fingers off the leather and then wraps his hand around mine again. He leans toward me so I can feel the heat of his body against my side. He talks to me softly. "The key is to get your mind off of things. Do you want to talk or do you want to listen?"

There's a slight jerk as the plane starts to pick up speed. The roar inside the cab is loud, and I clench my eyes shut. "Listen. I want to listen."

I lay my head back and listen to Ford talk. He jumps from one topic to another, and eventually, once we're up in the air, I can feel myself calm. He holds my hand the whole time, never letting me go. We joke about the first time we met and when I came in for the interview. I still can't believe he hired me without any experience, but he says he has a good sense about people. We talk about Ollie. We talk about his brothers. We talk so much that I'm surprised when I hear the pilot announce that we are about to land.

"You okay?" he asks me.

I blush, embarrassed. "Yeah, I'm good."

I pull my hand away, but he puts his finger on my chin and pulls my face toward him. "Don't do that."

"Do what?"

"Be embarrassed. You have nothing to be embarrassed about."

It amazes me that he knows exactly what I'm thinking without me having to say a word. "I bet you're thinking that I'm more trouble than I'm worth at this point."

He shakes his head. "You're no trouble at all, Lilian. Actually, I liked being able to be here for you."

Speechless, I watch as he unbuckles his seatbelt and stands up. "You coming, honey, or you want to hang here a little longer?"

I look out the window. "We landed?"

He chuckles. "Yep, we landed. Now let's get you off this plane so you can see Vegas."

We walk off the plane straight to a waiting car. As we ride down the road, Ford points out the window, giving me the breakdown on everything there is to see and do. There's so much to look at, but I find myself watching Ford instead of the passing sights.

FORD

I fucked up. That's what's going through my head as I swipe the key at the hotel room. I should have gotten separate rooms instead of a suite. I mean, sure, the suite is huge. It's two bedrooms that are separated by a kitchen and living room in between the bedrooms, but I don't think that's going to be enough. Just riding in the plane with her next to me was too much, and I couldn't keep my hands to myself. How did I think I would be able to resist the temptation of being in the same hotel room all weekend?

Already I've touched her way more than I should have. I had to keep reminding myself that I'm her boss, but that didn't stop me from holding her hand. Yeah, I told myself that I only did it so I could comfort her, but it's a lie. The fact is that if she's close to me, I want to touch her.

I open the door and hold it so she can pass through. She walks in, and I roll our bags behind us. "I hope this is okay, Lilian. If it makes you uncomfortable, you can have the suite and I can go downstairs to get another room."

She's walking around, and her mouth falls open. "What are you talking about, Ford? Geez, this is almost bigger than my whole house. There's plenty of room here."

I clear my throat and look around the big room. Yeah, it's big, but I don't think it's big enough. "I just don't want to make you feel uncomfortable, that's all."

She walks past me toward the patio door, smiling at me over her shoulder. "Uncomfortable? In a five-star hotel with turn-down service, three restaurants, room service and... a pool!" she squeals as she gets the door open. She points over her shoulder. "Ford, we have a private balcony that leads to a rooftop pool... and there's a hot tub."

I walk up behind her and love seeing the excitement on her face. "So I guess you approve then?"

She walks onto the patio. "I wish I'd brought a bathing suit."

I suck in a breath. Thinking of Lilian in a bathing

suit is not going to help me at all. I jerk my eyes off her ass when she turns back to me. She's shaking her head. "Forget that thought. We won't have time to swim."

The disappointment on her face has me commenting, "We can make time, and I'm sure they have bathing suits in the shop downstairs."

"No, it's fine. I'm sure they're a fortune. Plus, we're here to work." She passes by me on the way back into the suite. Her body glides against mine, and I suck in a breath on contact.

"You okay?"

I nod, walking back into the room, holding my hands in front of me. That's all I need is for her to see that I get a semi just from her rubbing against me. She's going to think I'm some old perv or something. "We have two hours before dinner with the Ogles. What would you like to do until then? Rest, go see some of the sights, go to the casino? You name it." Heck, anything to get out of these tight quarters. There's no way I'm going to keep my hands to myself this weekend. I obviously didn't think this through.

She reaches into the pocket of her jeans and pulls out a twenty dollar bill. "I've never gambled before, and I budgeted twenty dollars just for that."

"Sounds good. Let's go."

She doesn't budge, though. "Is dinner in the hotel?"

I nod.

She gestures to the dress pants and shirt I'm wearing and then toward her own jeans. "I'm going to go freshen up and change for dinner since we probably won't come back up before then. I won't be a minute."

She points around the room. "Which bedroom do you want?"

Fuck me just hearing her say *bed* has my dick coming alive. This was a terrible idea. "Either one. They both have their own bathroom, so pick whichever you want."

She smiles and rolls her suitcase to the bedroom. I grab mine and go in the opposite direction. I busy myself by unpacking to keep my thoughts off of Lilian in the next room naked. I'm sitting on the edge of my bed, counting down from a hundred when I hear Lilian call my name.

I take a deep breath and walk out of the bedroom with a forced smile on my face. My mouth drops when I see her, though. I've seen her dressed up before, but nothing like this. Her hair is swept up with tendrils framing her face. She has on a fitted dress that goes below her knees. It's very conservative but still sexy.

She tilts her head. "You okay?"

I nod. "Yes, I'm good. You ready?"

She grabs her purse off the counter and takes two steps before stopping and turning her back to me. "Shoot. Sorry, I couldn't get my zipper up. Can you help me?"

It's like a punch in the gut, taking my breath. She's positioned herself next to me, baring her back to me. My first thought is there's no bra strap. That's all I'll be thinking about the rest of the night. When I don't move—heck, I'm not even breathing—Lilian looks over her shoulder at me. "Ford?"

I move then, closer to her, lifting my hands to her dress. "Yeah, sorry."

I grab the zipper that starts at the curve of her ass. I know I shouldn't, but as I drag the material up, I let my knuckles caress her soft skin. She trembles, and goosebumps form on her arms. I take it slowly, and when I reach the top, I release the zipper and put my hands on her shoulders. Her whole body shudders, and I try to get myself under control. I'm her boss. She's too young for me. I shouldn't be doing this. I repeat these things over and over until I force myself to let her go and take a few steps backward. But no matter how far I go, I can still feel the softness of her skin under my fingers.

"Ready?" I ask in a strangled voice.

She clears her throat. "Yeah, I'm ready."

I follow behind her, wondering if she feels it too. Can she see a future between the two of us? My thoughts go back to the plane ride here. I understand how she's feeling about her sister, and I understand that she thinks she may have to leave, but what she doesn't realize is that I can't just let her go. There's no way I can let her leave. No, there has to be another way.

LILIAN

The last two hours Ford has taught me about gambling. I had some luck at the slot machine, and when I turned my twenty dollars into fifty, I knew I had to stop. Ford has stuck right by my side. He hasn't spent a penny, instead watching me the whole time. I figured he'd be bored, but every time I've looked at him, his face has been lit up like he's enjoying himself.

I look at the clock on the wall. "It's ten till. We should probably go." He looks disappointed that our time is up. "I feel bad you didn't get to gamble and were too busy showing me the ropes. We can come back after dinner."

He shakes his head as his hand fits across my lower

back. He's leading me toward the restaurant, and just like every other time he's touched me, I feel it everywhere. "I don't gamble. I'm not good at it. However, you are on a lucky streak. We can come back after dinner if you want to."

"No, I'm happy with my fifty dollars. But I do have to say, I can see how people find this addictive. It's a rush for sure."

We walk into the restaurant, and the hostess smiles at Ford.

"Hello. We have a reservation for four. It's under Ford Blaze."

The waitress looks Ford up and down with a smile. Jealousy shoots through me, and I step closer to him even though I know I don't have the right to.

"Right this way," she tells us.

We follow her, and Ford keeps his hand at my waist until we arrive at the table. He holds my seat out for me before taking his own and pulling me closer to him.

I try not to read anything into the way he's treating me. Ford has always been a good man. He opens doors, and he's always been attentive and kind. I shouldn't get my hopes up that this can be anything more than what it is. I'm here for work.

"Okay, so I made sure to look up Jim Ogle before we left. He's married to Victoria Ogle, and they've been married for fifteen years. He has fifteen stores in Nevada, and he seems happy with Blaze Whiskey since he's added it to every store he's opened in the last five years. His sales were down in the last quarter, but I'm not sure why. Every other store in the region has had at least a three percent increase."

He sits back in his chair, staring at me in awe. "I'm impressed."

I sit up a little straighter. "Thank you. I didn't want you to regret asking me to come. I think I've done everything I can to prepare for this dinner—and the conference—but I'll probably have questions."

He rises as an older couple comes toward us, but he leans down and whispers, "I'm happy I brought you, Lily. You have nothing to prove."

The way he shortened my name and the feel of his breath on my neck gives me a full body shiver. I feel a warmth spread in my lower belly as he rises up to shake hands. "Jim, I'm so glad we could get together before tomorrow. And Victoria, it's so good to see you again."

I stand up, still recovering from Ford's confession. I shake hands with the Ogles before we all sit down. The conversation runs smoothly, and Jim seems to be an interesting story teller. If nothing else, he likes to hear himself talk.

However, I'm surprised when he openly starts

flirting with the waitress. Victoria's face turns red, and she looks down at the menu she's holding. I look back at Jim as if I totally misinterpreted what he was doing. Surely, that's the case.

We order our meals, but an uneasiness has settled over me, and I grow quiet. Poor Victoria is trying to seem unfazed, but it's obvious that she's upset. I try to bring her into the conversation. "Victoria, do you have any children?"

Jim finishes off his glass of whiskey and slams it noisily on the table. "We sure do. Eighteen years ago and she still hasn't lost the baby weight."

I gasp. No he didn't just say that.

Ford tenses beside me, and I don't know what to say to that. With a red face, Victoria smiles softly at me, ignoring her husband. "We have one son. Mitchell is graduating high school this year, and he plans to go to college on the East Coast. I had hoped he was going to pick somewhere closer, but he wants to spread his wings."

I give her a warm smile. "I raised my sister, and she recently got married. It's hard having them leave home. I miss having her around the house."

Victoria smiles in understanding. We continue talking, and at this point, I don't even care that I'm not including her husband in the conversation. I catch

Victoria nervously watching him as he throws back another drink. The more he drinks, the more nervous she gets.

Even Ford notices it. He tilts his drink toward the man sitting across from him. "Jim, you better slow down and leave some for the rest of us."

Jim laughs out loud obnoxiously. "We won't be running out. I'm having dinner with the man that makes my favorite whiskey."

Ford's smile is tight. Most people wouldn't realize it, but I know him pretty well, and it's obvious that his patience is wearing thin.

Luckily, the waitress brings our plates and walks around the table setting them down. I hold my breath, waiting for Jim to hit on her again, but he doesn't. I breathe a sigh of relief when she walks away.

I point at Victoria's plate of pasta. "Oh, Victoria, that looks good. What is it called again?"

Jim looks over at his wife's plate. "I told you to get the salad."

She puts her fork into the pasta. "I didn't want the salad." She lifts her eyes to mine, and I see the defiance darkening them. "This is pasta alla Norma. It has eggplant in it." She tilts the plate toward me. "Do you want to try it?"

Jim interrupts her. "Give it to her and I'll order you the salad."

"Jim." Ford interrupts him. "I think that's enough. You're making the whole table uncomfortable."

Jim just laughs. "No, everyone's uncomfortable because it's obvious she shouldn't be eating that. She's too fat."

Victoria gasps, and I don't even think before I hit my full glass of wine, knocking it over right into Jim's plate. The splash makes it up onto his jacket.

Before I can even pull my hand back, Jim has his hand wrapped around my wrist. Ford stands up and leans over in Jim's face. "Let her go, Jim."

Because Jim doesn't do it fast enough, his tone is low and lethal. "Now."

Jim's face is scrunched up in anger, and when he releases me, I pull my hand back.

Ford grabs Jim by the front of his shirt and pulls him out of his seat. The whole restaurant goes quiet, and people are watching with interest.

I put my hand on Ford's back. "Ford, he's not worth it. Please don't."

Ford reaches back, and I wrap my hand around his. He looks at the other woman. "Will you be okay, Victoria?"

She nods. "I always am."

Ford nods in understanding and then leans down in Jim's face. I can't hear what he says, but when he releases his hold on him, Jim's eyes are huge. Ford gently pulls me away from the table. We stop at the hostess stand, and Ford leaves cash for the bill. We walk across the casino and then ride up the elevator to the top floor. Neither Ford nor I have said another word to each other, but I can feel the anger radiating off him.

That man was despicable. There's no way I could sit there another minute with him. I glance at Ford, and his jaw is pulled tight. In the two years I've worked for him, I haven't seen him this mad before.

I shouldn't have come.

I open my mouth but close it quickly. What am I going to say? Should I apologize for dumping my drink on that guy when I feel no remorse at all? I can't. Instead, I slam my mouth shut and wrap my arms around my middle. As soon as the elevator dings, Ford holds his hand out for me to go through.

I walk quickly down the hallway to our suite. He gave me a key earlier, and I have it out of my purse and in my hand when I get to the door. I open it and don't stop walking until I'm in my room with the door closed behind me.

Pacing back and forth, all I can think about is that

poor woman. I should have done something for her. I
don't know what, but something.

There's a knock at the door, and I take a deep
breath before sitting on the edge of the chair in the
corner of the room. This is where he fires me.
"Come in."

Ford

I open the door, and when I see Lilian sitting on the chair in the corner, I walk over and drop to my knees in front of her. I reach for her hand, pressing the ice wrapped in the towel against her wrist. Seeing the red marks on her delicate skin has me seething all over again.

I feel like I can't catch my breath. I should have killed Jim instead of walking away like I did.

"This was a bad idea. I shouldn't have come, Ford." She seems to weigh her words before blurting. "I'm sorry that I pissed you off. I just couldn't sit there and watch him treat her like that."

I pull back. "You think I'm mad at you?"

She won't look at me as she shrugs her shoulders. She looks so sad. I lean toward her, putting my finger on her chin and pulling her face to me. "Look at me, Lily."

Sadness fills her eyes, and I don't know what to do to make it right. "Oh honey, I'm not mad at you at all. When he touched you, I wanted to kill him. He had no right..."

My voice is thick with emotion, and I clench my eyes shut, trying to get the image of Jim grabbing Lilian out of my head.

Her hand touches my shoulder, and she squeezes me. "Ford, I'm fine, though."

I look at her. "He shouldn't have touched you."

She pulls the towel from her hand and sets it on the floor beside us before holding her wrist out to me. "Look, it's fine."

I run my finger over the red marks on her skin. "I should have killed him."

She gasps. "Don't talk that way. I'm not worried about him. I'm worried about Victoria. I have to help her, Ford. I have to."

I nod. "We can talk to her tomorrow, or if you want to call her tonight, I have her number saved in my phone."

She grabs my wrist. "Oh please, can I? I won't sleep at all if I don't know she's all right."

I find Victoria's number in my phone and hit dial.

She answers on the second ring. "Hi, Victoria, this is Ford. I hope it's okay we called. Lilian would like to talk to you, but if this is a bad time—"

"This is fine. Put her on."

I hand the phone to Lilian, and she quickly puts it to her ear. I only hear one side of the conversation. Lilian doesn't say much except to ask her if she's okay, and then by the end of the phone call, Lilian's eyes are wide, and she's telling her goodbye.

"Everything okay?"

She nods. "What did you do, Ford?"

I don't have to ask her what she means. "It's okay."

She's shaking her head. "You can't cancel all contracts between Blaze Whiskey and the Ogle stores." She puts her head in her hands. "Oh no, Ford. Do you know how much that's going to cost you? Geez, Lucas is going to be so mad I'm the reason you guys lost this contract. You don't have to do that, Ford. Call him back."

I grip on to her shoulders. I'm holding her too tightly, and I force myself to loosen my hold. "First of all, Lucas is not going to be mad. When he knows what... happened, he'll back up my decision. And second, you need to know this right now. I will never be okay with someone treating you like that man did back there."

"But…"

I cut her off. "No buts. Was Victoria okay?"

She nods. "She has everything in place already. She was leaving him after their son graduated, but she's moving it up now. And get this, she'll get half of all the stores."

"Good. When it's all said and done, we'll give her our business. I'll never do business with Jim again."

She breathes out a sigh of relief, and she seems happy, but I can't get over the guilt I feel. "I'm selfish, Lily. If I hadn't brought you, this wouldn't have happened."

She searches my eyes. "Why did you bring me?" When I don't answer immediately, she says, "I mean, in two years, you've never brought me on a business trip. Never asked me to come. Why now?"

I suck in a breath. "I don't know if you want to hear this or not, Lily."

She nods. "I do."

I know that what I say next can change everything. But even knowing that, I can't keep it to myself any longer. "For the last two years—since the day I hired you—I've had feelings for you. You said you didn't date and now, out of the blue, you're dating. I want to be the one you go on dates with."

A soft gasp escapes her, and she looks at me in shock. "You want to date me?"

Fuck, there's more I want to do with her, but I figure I've surprised her enough. I lean forward and lower my voice. "Yes. I want to date you."

She's speechless, and it's obvious she doesn't know what to say. I turn her wrist over in my hand before lifting it and pressing my lips to the slight red marks there. "I'm sorry about your wrist, honey. Good night."

I lay her arm in her lap, forcing myself to get up and walk away. I'm almost through the door when I hear her soft voice. "That's it? You're going to drop that bombshell on me and then what? Walk away?"

I grip the door frame and turn to look at her. Fuck, she's so beautiful it takes my breath away just looking at her. "Yes, I brought you here, and you're dealing with a lot of shit, Lily. There's no pressure. Think about it. There's no rush or deadline with us. I'll see you in the morning."

I get halfway across the suite and then stop. Walking away is not what I want to do. I want to hold her in my arms and show her exactly what I've thought about doing to her these last two years. I want her to know that this isn't some fling... that I don't want to just date her. I want her in my life in every way possible. I want everything she's willing to give.

I turn on my heel to go back to her, and the image of Jim Ogle grabbing her wrist fills my head. My whole body tenses, and my hands fist at my side. She needs time. So much has happened today, and I know she needs time to process it all.

I walk toward the door to the suite and walk out into the hallway. The temptation to go to her is too much, and I know I need to put some distance between us before I do something foolish. I don't drink a lot, but I can use one right now.

LILIAN

I tossed and turned most of the night. Since I was eighteen, I've done the right thing. I was responsible, and I tried to base every decision on how it would affect Carrie. I don't blame her by any means for the decisions I made. I knew what I had to do, and I did it. But if there's ever a time to start living for myself and what I want, it's now.

I get ready the next morning with determination. Now if I can just keep this attitude all day, I'll have it made.

With a smile on my face, I walk into living room of the suite. It only takes a moment for me to realize that I'm alone. "Ford," I call out.

When there's no answer, I look around the room and notice the silver domed plates set up on the table.

Instead of going to the food, I walk to the edge of the living room area and stand in the open doorway of Ford's room. His cologne fills the air, and I breathe it in. I've always appreciated his manly scent that reminds me of being outside in the sunshine. "Ford," I call out to the empty room.

The bed is made, and everything is tidy. I turn back out of the room before I do something crazy like roll around in the spot he slept in last night or lay my head down on his pillow. When back in the living room, I spot the note on the counter.

I pick it up and instantly recognize the small, neat writing on the hotel notepad.

> LILY,
> I WENT DOWN EARLY TO TRY AND MEET UP WITH A FEW CLIENTS. I'LL SEE YOU AT THE CONFERENCE. I ORDERED YOU SOME BREAKFAST. I ALSO HAD THE GIFT SHOP BRING UP TWO SWIMMING SUITS. I'M SURE YOU CAN FIND TIME TO SWIM WHILE YOU'RE HERE. SEE YOU SOON. CALL ME IF YOU NEED ANYTHING.
> FORD

I read the note again, trying to analyze it and see if

I can read anything more into it than what's already on the paper. He called me Lily instead of Lilian, which is something. The shortened nickname is new, and I like hearing it from him.

I'm not surprised that he ordered me breakfast or the fact he had swimsuits brought up from the gift shop. He's always been considerate and would probably do the same for anyone.

As I sit down and uncover the domed plates, I grab a piece of toast and nibble on it, lost in thought. Could he have changed his mind since last night? Maybe he has thought about it, and he doesn't want to date me. I mean, us together is probably not the best idea. Could I work for him if it doesn't work out?

Damn. Somehow I've already ruined things before I even agreed to anything.

Unable to eat anything else, I pour a cup of coffee and start rounding up everything I need for the conference today. After stuffing a bottle of water, some mints, and my laptop into my tote bag, I look at myself in the mirror to make sure I look the part of Ford Blaze's assistant. I slide my hand down my thighs. I'm wearing a skirt and low heels with a tucked-in blouse. Pulling my phone from my purse, I see I have fifteen minutes before the conference starts, so I make my way downstairs.

After picking up my registration packet, I make it through the rows of vendors. I pass by the booths and walk straight to the safety class. There are five classes that I'm attending today, even skipping lunch to try to get them all in.

I sit down at the table and take out my laptop, ready to learn. I really don't want to let Ford down or for him to regret bringing me. Especially after everything with last night, I feel like I need to do a good job.

The first two classes, I stay in my seat as the speakers switch to other classrooms. I have ten pages of notes by the end of the second class. When I get up to go to the next one, I grab a protein bar off the refreshment cart and then quickly find my seat.

"You doing okay?"

My whole body tenses as Ford slides into the chair next to mine.

I lift my eyes to his, trying to read the look he's giving me. "Yeah, how are you?"

He looks tired, and I curl my fingers into my palm to resist reaching up and touching him.

He shrugs, watching me. "I didn't sleep very well."

I groan inwardly. "I'm sure you didn't. Most people wouldn't when they lose an account that's going to cost them a few hundred thousand dollars."

His face transforms in front of me. "Stop, Lily. I

don't want to hear anything else about it. Do you understand that I don't want to do business with a man like that?"

"Yeah, but your brothers—"

"My brothers don't want to do business with a man like that either. You know us, you know all of us. Well, besides Huddy. But hell, he'd probably feel as strong about it as I do, and none of it was your fault."

I nod. The way he's protective of me has heat flaring in my chest. I'm about to tell him what I've been thinking about half the night and all morning. I'd like to talk more about what he told me last night, but before I can muster up the courage to say anything, the woman at the front of the room starts talking.

I give Ford a regretful look and turn to the front, pulling out my laptop. I start typing notes when I notice Ford write something down on his notepad.

He holds it out in front of me. *Want to meet for lunch after this?*

I type onto my computer and point to it. "Can't. I'm skipping it so I don't miss the class on new methods of distilling."

He gives me an unhappy look, but I don't ask him anything about it. I just keep working.

He disappears halfway through the presentation, and later when I get to the final talk of the day, Ford is waiting for me with a small Tupperware bowl set out in front of him.

"Eat," he tells me before I even sit down.

I look around, and there are other people with plates of food. "Are you going to eat with me?"

He shakes his head. "Nope. I had lunch with the Milton brothers from Texas. I'm sending them a contract to be signed when we get back."

I don't even try to hide my excitement. "The Milton brothers? THE Milton Brothers?"

He laughs. "Yes. They are probably three times the size of Ogle."

I grab on to his forearm. "Ford! That's amazing. How did you—?"

I cut off when the next speaker comes to the podium. I lean over and whisper to him, "I can't wait to hear all about it."

He leans forward, and his hot breath caresses my cheek. "I'll tell you anything you want to know, but first you eat. I got you your favorite comfort food."

It's then that I really inspect the plate in front me. I peel back the lid and gasp at the ooey-gooey macaroni and cheese that is still steaming hot. I take the fork he's holding and dig in, moaning as the first taste hits my tongue. Either I'm starving or this is the best macaroni and cheese I've ever eaten. "Mmmmm, this is good."

He's watching my mouth, nodding his head.

I smile at him, wondering what he's thinking about. "Thank you for the food. I was hungry."

He nods and dips his hand into his suit pocket, pulling out a handful of peppermint patties. My eyes light up. Peppermint patties are my weakness. "Oh gah," I whisper. "I could kiss you right now."

I don't even think about it when I say it. I hold my hand out, and he puts the chocolate in my palm before grabbing my wrist. "If we weren't here of all places, I'd take you up on that."

I fight the overwhelming need to lean forward and press my lips to his. "Deal."

His eyes flare, and his voice is husky. "I'm going to hold you to that, Lily."

I nod, biting onto my lower lip. Geez, just thinking about kissing him has me twitching in my seat. He finally releases me and points a finger to my food. "Eat."

I nod, picking up the fork and piercing a noodle before bringing it to my lips.

I get through the class, and afterward, Ford and I walk around to all the vendor booths. We stay in the same aisle, each talking to different people.

"Hey." I turn on my heel, and for the first time today, I see Victoria.

I touch her arm. "Hey, how are you? Everything okay?"

I can't help but look around for her husband and spot Ford while doing so. He's stepped away from the man he was talking to and is watching Victoria and me. He looks around, no doubt looking for Jim like I am.

"Oh, wow, everything is great. I know how uncomfortable last night had to be for you and Ford, but I needed it. It's what finally convinced me that I was doing the right thing. Even though it was mortifying."

Her cheeks are red, hinting at her embarrassment, but besides that, she seems to be glowing with her decision. "Don't even think twice about it. I'm so happy for you, and if you ever want to talk, you can call me anytime."

Impulsively, I lean in and hug her. She squeezes me tightly, and we stand here in the middle of the aisle embracing. When she finally pulls back, she's laughing and wiping at a tear on her cheek. "Oh, I guess I needed that." She squeezes my hand. "Lilian, you are a gem. Thank you. I'll be talking to you soon."

I nod and watch her walk away. She stops and talks to Ford, and he hugs her as well. She's blushing like a schoolgirl when she walks away from him.

His eyes are on me, and he weaves through the people to get to me. "You okay?"

I bend one knee, holding my foot up behind me. "I'm good. My feet are feeling it, though. I'm not used to all this walking and standing."

He grabs my tote bag and slings it over his shoulder.

I smile at the image of him with what looks like a purse over his shoulder. It doesn't faze him, though. He laces his arm through mine. "Come on. Let's go."

I don't resist, falling into step beside him. "Where are we going?"

"Uh, to freshen up. Then you can pick what you want to do tonight. You've never been to Vegas. You want to sightsee, gamble, take in a show, dinner... you pick."

Without even thinking, I groan. "I'd like to order in and go swimming."

He punches the button on the elevator, and we wait. I'm sure he probably wants to go out. I shouldn't be such a stick in the mud. I'm about to tell him we can do whatever he wants, when the doors open. Three women are getting off on this floor, and they're all dressed up. They are giggling and having a good time until they all get quiet when they see Ford. He releases me as we walk onto the elevator, his hand going to my waist. If he notices the women staring at him, he doesn't act like it. Instead, he's watching me. "You pushed yourself too hard today. You shouldn't have skipped lunch."

I put my hand to my still full belly. On top of the big bowl of mac and cheese, I ate all three of the peppermint patties. "Uh, if I'd done that, I wouldn't have gotten the best macaroni and cheese in Nevada, so I'd say I'm winning." I put my hand on his forearm. "But really, we can go out. Give me a few minutes to get ready, and we can go paint the town."

He leans down, leveling me with a look. "I thought you wanted to stay in."

I shrug, avoiding his gaze. "It's fine. You're right. I haven't seen Vegas, and I'm sure you don't want to be holed up in a hotel room all night."

The elevator stops on our floor, and we walk off down the hallway. Ford has my tote with my key card, so I wait for him to unlock the door with the card from his wallet. As soon as we're inside, he sets my tote down on the chair and turns to me, his hands to my upper arms. "Don't do that."

I shake my head not understanding. "Don't do what?"

He brushes my hair away from my face and searches my eyes. "You're always doing what other people want. For the first time, you need to do what you want. There's no expectations. I've been to Vegas plenty of times. You get to pick what we do."

I shake my head. "Ford—"

He cuts me off. "Nope. Seriously. Look me in the eyes."

I tilt my head back to look at him.

"Good." He nods approvingly. "Now if you could do anything right now, what would you do?"

I blow out a breath. "Are you sure about this?"

He nods, giving me a look as if he's daring me not to obey. "Fine. If I could do anything right now, I'd take off these shoes...."

He doesn't hesitate. He drops down to one knee and reaches for my foot, lifting it to slide my foot out of my shoe. "Ford, you don't have to—" I start, but he doesn't listen. He lifts my other foot and removes that shoe as well.

He rises to his feet with a satisfied smile on his face. "Now what?"

Oh God. I wish I could tell him what I really want right now. I'd love for him to pick me up and carry me to the bedroom. My heart flutters in my chest when I name the next best thing. It's no match, but still good. "Swimming... and then room service."

He squeezes my upper arms. "Done. Go get your suit on."

He steps away from me and is walking toward his bedroom. "Are you joining me?"

He stops and turns to me. "I was going to, but I don't have to."

I croak, "Yes!" Heat floods my face, but I clear my throat and try it again. "I was hoping you'd swim too."

He nods. "See you out there."

I wait until he disappears into his room before making my way to my bedroom. The bathing suits are still in the bag, and I dump them out on the bed. One is a black one piece. It's very conservative. The other suit is a white two piece. I hold the two in my hands and feel as if these two suits are a metaphor for my life. I could take the safe route and wear the black suit that covers my body. Or I can wear the white two piece that shows more skin and is a little bit more adventurous.

I drop the black suit and start pulling tags off the white one. It's about time I try on the new me.

FORD

"How's it going, buddy?"

I was so excited to meet Lilian at the pool that I completely forgot about my nightly call to Ollie. Now as I lean against the edge of the hot tub, I'm talking to my child, hoping that he doesn't hear the splash of the water or the roar of the hot tub jets.

"Dad! Lucas and Issi took me to ride go-carts! We went to the arcade too."

"Wow! That sounds fun, Ollie."

"It was, and guess what?" He doesn't wait for me to guess before he continues, "I beat Uncle Lucas. He was so slowwwww."

"He's always been slow. So you're having fun?"

"Yes!" he screams into the phone.

I lean my elbows onto the side of the hot tub with the phone to my ear. "Are you being good for Uncle Lucas and Aunt Isabella?"

"Daaad, I'm always good."

I laugh, but the truth is, he is normally a good kid. I don't know how I got so lucky in that department. "I'll be home tomorrow night, Ollie."

"K, Dad. I gotta go. I love you."

I barely get out "I love you" before I hear the click on the phone. The sound of Lilian getting in the water has me turning around.

"Was that Ollie? Is he having fun?"

She is walking down the few steps of the hot tub, but the water is only up to her knees. She leans over, gliding her hand along the top of the water, and I take a step toward her. How can I not? She's so tempting, and she draws me in even though I know I should be keeping my distance.

She's watching me, her eyes on my chest, and I don't stop until I'm right in front of her. "I probably should have told the gift shop to get you something that covers a little more."

Her chin lifts defiantly. "The other one was a modest black one piece, but I chose this one. If it bothers you—"

I cut her off, wrapping my hand around her waist

and pulling her to me. "It doesn't bother me, Lilian. Not like you mean. My only thought is that we are in a public place, and I don't want other men to see you like this."

She looks around the edge of the hot tub and the pool. There are six rooms that have balconies to the private pool area, but every one of those balconies are empty. I'm not a fool. When she said she wanted to go swimming, I rented the other five rooms to keep this pool private.

But the joke's on me. Her hand goes to my phone, and she takes it, walking backward to set it on the edge of the hot tub before making her way back in front of me. Her hand burns into my chest as she curls her fingers against me, giving my hair there a little tug. "Try again, Ford. You think I don't know? I've worked with you for two years, and I know that you booked those rooms and that there is no one staying in them."

She gives me a knowing look and asks, "So tell me, why should I have a more modest bathing suit on?"

I can no longer keep my hands to myself. I run my finger under the strap of her suit at her shoulder. She visibly trembles, and I cup both her shoulders in my palms. "Because I want you. I've wanted you for two years, and being this close to you, seeing you like this…" I blow out a breath and try to control my breathing. "It's too tempting, Lily. Way too tempting."

Her eyes are searching mine, and I try hard not to put my guard up. There are so many reasons why this is a bad idea. I'm her boss. She just wants to have fun and is not looking for anything serious. My son is already attached to her, and I can't let him get hurt, but knowing all that, I still can't walk away from her.

The beginning of a smile tips her lips, and her hands slide up my chest to cup behind my neck. I let my hands slide to her back, pulling her flush against me.

She keeps looking at my lips, and finally she murmurs huskily to me. "I owe you a kiss, Ford."

At first, I don't get her meaning, and then I remember her saying she could kiss me for bringing her food. I know it's a game, and she doesn't owe me anything, but I'm not going to refuse it. Not when I've been dying to have her lips on mine.

"I do remember you saying something about that."

Her breasts are flattened to my chest, and I can feel her shakily inhale with each breath she takes. Being this close to her is having the same effect on me. We're so close, all I have to do is lean forward a few inches and I would have her lips against mine.

I bring my hand up to cup her neck, her pulse racing under my thumb. "Ford, please?"

Her pleading with me is my undoing.

I've thought about this every moment since she kissed me the other night, and there is no way I'm not going to savor it. I want to ravage her, but I do my best to take it slow and enjoy it. But fuck, her lips under mine make me lose the last bit of control I'm holding on to. She wraps her arms around my neck, and I tilt my head to deepen the kiss.

Her body is pressed against mine, but she's not close enough. It will never be enough.

I slide my tongue into her mouth, and she whimpers. My hands are everywhere, sliding up and down her back, and when she raises her legs around my hips, I cup her ass, holding her to me.

My cock is hard, pressed against her core. The only thing between us is the tiny bit of material between her legs and my thin shorts. Whether she realizes it or not, she's lifting her hips, pressing closer to me, trying to get my engorged cock at her entrance. The heated water surrounds us, and I feel as if I'm on fire, but I'm not stopping.

I pull away from her lips and bury my face in her neck. I'm kissing every bare inch of skin I can reach, and I pull the strap down her shoulder, exposing her breast. She fits perfectly in my palm, and I pluck her nipple between my thumb and forefinger. She moans as she rocks her hips, arching her back, pressing her breast into my hand. "I need you, Lilian."

No sooner are the words out of my mouth then my phone rings. I ignore it as I trail kisses down her collarbone, making my way to her bare breast.

"It's Lucas."

"Ignore it," I groan.

Her hands go to my shoulders. "Ford, Ollie's with him. It could be important."

"Fuck!" I curse, knowing she's right. She's unlatching her legs from around me and on the other side of the hot tub by the time I catch my breath and answer the phone that is on the other side of the tub. "Yeah?"

"Dad! Tomorrow a bunch of my friends are going to the park to play soccer and have a cookout. Can I go?"

My eyes are on Lilian, and she's staring at me with her eyes wide. My voice sounds calmer than what I'm feeling. "If I'm home in time, we can go, okay?"

"Lucas and Issi said they'd take me if you weren't home. Can I go, Dad? Please."

"Sure."

"Thanks, Dad. Love you."

He hangs up the phone, and I don't have to wonder if we're going to pick up where we left off. Lilian has pulled her swimsuit back up and is climbing out of the hot tub. She goes straight to the pool, diving in and starting to swim laps. I take my time, waiting until it's not painful for me to walk. Fuck, two years of blue balls suck.

I stand at the edge of the pool and watch her quietly. I know she's trying to work through some things, and I need to be patient even if it's the last thing I want to do.

Finally, after what feels like forever, she swims toward me and holds on to the side of the pool. I sit down on the edge, dangling my feet beside her.

"Ford, uh, I..."

When she stops, the look on her face tells me everything I need to know. "You don't want this."

She doesn't deny it, but she still looks hesitant. "I just don't think it is a good idea."

I know exactly what she's thinking. It's the same thing I've used to talk myself out of approaching her the last two years. I'm her boss, and she's off limits.

I shrug, acting as if I'm unfazed by it all when in fact I'm not handling it well at all. "I understand. I'm not going to force you into anything."

"Ford..." she starts, dragging my name out.

I hold my hand up to stop her. "It's fine, Lilian. I get it. I don't like it, but I get it. I'm going to go in and order dinner and shower. What would you like to eat?"

"Nothing. I'm not very hungry."

I don't argue with her. She may say nothing, but I'm going to order something for her. I've watched her for two years. I know what she likes and how she likes it. "Okay, it should be here in thirty minutes or so. Enjoy your swim."

I push myself up and walk into our room from the balcony. It takes everything I have not to turn around to beg and plead with her to reconsider.

LILIAN

I may have told Ford I wasn't hungry, but halfway through my swim, he came outside holding up a domed plate of food. He set it on the table on the patio and called out to me. "Food. Just in case you're hungry."

"Thanks" is the only thing I say when there's a few hundred things I want to be saying to him. I fucked up. I know I did. I freaked out when Ollie called. I felt like maybe that was fate or something telling me we shouldn't be doing this. But now all I feel is deep regret.

I climb out of the pool and dry off, wrapping myself in the towel. I make my way to the patio seat, peeking inside to see if Ford is eating at the table there. I can't see him, and I figure it's just as well.

Curious, I pull off the dome lid and am surprised by the meal in front of me. It's definitely not a normal meal for Vegas, and I know that Ford ordered it specifically because he knows I love it. It's my favorite, a fried green tomato sandwich with bacon, lettuce and—I peel back the bread—Dijon mustard instead of mayonnaise. It always amazes me when he does stuff like this. He knows what I like.

I eat half the sandwich, lost in thought. The sun is starting to set, but the lights from downtown are beautiful from here.

I eat what I can of the sandwich and then sit back, lost in thought.

It's only when I'm sitting in silence that I start to get antsy. I shouldn't have walked away. I know I shouldn't have.

I pick up the plate and carry it inside. I search around the room for Ford, and I assume he's in the shower when I hear the water running in there.

I go to my own room, peeling off the bathing suit and then taking my own shower. I take my time, trying to relax, but I'm a bundle of nerves.

I shouldn't have stopped what was happening.

As the water slides down my body, my skin tingles just remembering how it felt to have Ford's hands on me. How long have I thought about it, imagined it, dreamt about it? Dang, since the first day I've met him, I've wondered what it would be like.

I had the opportunity in my hands, and I let it slip away. I'm a fool. A damn fool.

Since I was eighteen, I've done the right thing. Whatever was expected or needed of me, I've done it. He's my boss, and I shouldn't sleep with him. But for the first time ever, I don't want to do what's right. I want to do what I want.

I take my time in the shower. I lotion my entire body. I dry my hair and let my mind wander. But no matter how I look at it, I know I can't let this go. I can't leave here tomorrow without giving in to what I want.

I find the hotel robe on the back of my bathroom door. Putting it over my bare body, I cinch it around my waist and walk into the living room. Quietly, I stand here and listen. The shower is no longer running, but I peek into his room and it's empty. The patio door is open a few inches, and when I look outside, I see his legs spread out in front of him.

Taking a deep breath, I push the door the rest of the way open. He's drinking a beer, looking out into the night. "Ford."

He takes a deep breath, and I expect to hear impatience in his voice, but I don't. "Yeah, honey, you okay?"

I move to stand in front of him. He has a pair of shorts on and nothing else. He's beautiful just like this, and in this instant, I know I'm doing the right thing. "I want you, Ford. I shouldn't have stopped us earlier."

His voice is gruff, but he leans forward, setting the beer on the table beside him. "Why did you stop, Lily? You don't owe me anything. Hell, honey, you don't even owe me a reason. If you don't want—"

I cut him off because I figure it's the only way to get my point across. "I do though. I do want you."

I undo the tie at my waist and then let the robe fall to the ground around me. His eyes travel up and down my body. His breathing becomes labored, and he sucks in a deep breath. "Fuck, you're beautiful."

I reach for him. "Ford, please, I'm tired of always doing the right thing. I want this to happen. Please... please don't make me wait anymore."

He's on his feet in an instant. His body is pressed against mine, and I can feel the hard bulge of his manhood pressed against my belly. I lean into him, but his hands go to my upper arms, trying to keep me at a distance. "Are you sure, Lily? We don't have to do this."

I suck in a breath and try not to let my insecurity

take me under. The truth is, Ford could have any woman he wanted. He's a beautiful, generous, caring man. I know I'm probably not his usual type, but that doesn't matter right now because I feel the proof of his desire. I jut my chin at him with a challenge. "I want you, Ford. I got caught up earlier in what's right and what's wrong, but the truth is, I can't live with myself if I walk away. I've never..." I suck in a breath, hating the vulnerability I'm feeling but knowing I need to get it out. "I've never wanted anyone as much as I want you. Working with you day after day. Wishing and hoping for just one look, one touch, and one kiss. Please, Ford. Even if it's only one night, I want it.... I want you."

His hands go to my waist, and he lifts me up. I wrap my legs around him as he turns and presses my back against the wall. The feel of the cool stone has me trembling, but I'm not cold for long. It's like Ford has been caged up for months and is finally set free. I feel him everywhere. His hands caress my naked body while his mouth moves savagely across my skin. I tilt my hips toward his, and his erection hits me where I need him most. The moan that escapes me is loud and fills the silence around us. He jerks back to look at me, and my cheeks heat in embarrassment. It's like I have no control around him.

He steps away from the wall and lets me slide down his body. When my feet hit the ground, he bends over to pick up the robe. I panic for an instant, wondering if this is some kind of payback and he's going to send me packing.

But instead, he lays the robe on the chair he stood up from and sets me down on top of it. His knees hit the ground with a thud, but he doesn't wince or act as if it hurts. He's a man on a mission.

He puts his hand on my chest, pushing me back before taking hold of my knees and spreading my legs apart. He positions his shoulders, holding me open while his hands slide up my thighs. My hips rise in anticipation, and he smiles at me, knowing that he already has me on the very edge of control and it's not going to take much for me to topple over.

He leans in and presses his nose to my pussy. With a deep inhale, his body shudders. "Fuck, you smell good."

"Ford, please," I beg him.

He doesn't make me wait. His finger strokes through my slick, wet folds, and he groans. "You're soaked, baby. Fuck, you're going to feel so good wrapped around my dick."

His words are muffled, but I hear him before he dives in, licking me, tasting me, suckling me like an obsessed man that was just handed everything he wants.

With each stroke of his tongue across my clit, my body shakes. He's relentless, and when I can't take it any longer, he pumps two fingers into me while he sucks my clit into his mouth. I grab on to the arms of the chair and squeeze as an orgasm wracks through my body.

He doesn't let up. It's like he wants everything I'm willing to give. He brings me to the edge again, and with one hand, I wrap my fingers around his hair. I don't know if I'm trying to pull him away or hold him to me. Maybe a little bit of both because what he's doing to my body is too intense and all-consuming.

I can't hold it in. The scream is loud, and my body jerks uncontrollably as another orgasm takes over.

FORD

Knowing that it's my name she's shouting as I give her pleasure is like nothing I've felt before. She's barely recovered from the two orgasms and I'm lifting her up, pressing my mouth to hers. Her orgasm coats my chin and beard, but she doesn't seem to mind it. Her tiny whimpers and the way she's rocking her body against mine tells me she likes the taste of herself on my tongue.

I lift her easily from the chair. I may have blocked the rooms on this floor, but I still don't want to chance anyone hearing her satisfied moans. That sound is only for me. No one else.

I carry her inside, using my foot to close the sliding door. As soon as it's shut behind us, I carry Lily to my bedroom and lay her back on the bed.

She's watching me through hooded eyes, and I'm breathing like I just ran a mile. I'm completely on edge, and I know it's only because I need to be inside her. Nothing in me is going to be settled or satisfied until I've claimed her completely.

I lean over her, searching her eyes. "I need to be inside you, Lily. I don't want to wait, and I don't want anything between us."

She seems dazed as she nods her head.

I put my hand on the side of her face, rubbing my thumb along her jawline. "I want to feel you, Lily. I want to feel you clamp down on me... I want it all."

She nods, blinking.

Fuck. "Lily, honey, tell me if you're okay with this."

She nods. "I'm on birth control, and I'm clean."

My hips jerk because she's giving me the okay. I'm so hard right now, I struggle getting my shorts down over my erect manhood. "I'm clean. I haven't been with anyone in two years... since I met you."

I don't know why I said it, but I wanted her to know. She needs to know that I haven't even looked at another woman since she walked into Blaze Whiskey.

I see the second that she gets the gist of what I'm saying. Her eyes widen, and she raises up on her elbows. "Two years? You haven't—"

I shake my head. "Not since I laid eyes on you, Lily. There's no way I could."

Her mouth drops, and she closes it quickly before shaking her head in disbelief. "But all the women that hit on you, that ask you out, that practically chase you—"

I cut her off with a kiss. It's a kiss that's meant to make her forget about all that. I saw the pain in her eyes when she was talking about those other women. I wish I could make her understand that no one matters to me but her.

I reluctantly end the kiss and rest my forehead on hers. "I don't want to think about anyone or anything except for this right here. Me and you, Lily. Right now, that's all that matters to me."

I see the question in her eyes, but she doesn't put voice to it. I put my palm at her pussy and whisper to her, "Now are you going to let me claim you? Take you like I want to?"

She nods, letting out a pant of breath.

I shake my head. "Words, Lily. Tell me."

Her voice is husky. "Yes, Ford. I want you inside me. I want to make you feel what you've made me feel. I want to feel you inside me, and I want to be the one you're thinking of when you lose control."

"Fuck." I grind out the word between my clenched

teeth. Just hearing her talk that way has my balls drawing up and cum leaking from my tip.

I draw her knees up and position myself at her entrance. I push into her slowly, taking my time, wanting to revel in it all, but I can't hold back. As soon as I feel her channel tightening around me, I want to thrust my hips and stake my claim on her. Every muscle in my body is pulled tight as I try to hold myself back.

She lifts her hips, and her heels dig into my back. "Yes," she moans. "Please, Ford. Don't stop."

I grunt in agreement, but I can't get any words out. There's no way I can stop now. I've felt her pussy, warm and soft, wrapped around my dick. No, I won't be stopping until she's coming on my dick and screaming my name again.

I push a little more into her, and she huffs in frustration. "Don't hold back, Ford. I want to see you lose control... I want all of you, exactly how you are."

I groan loudly as I thrust my hips forward. Her pussy spasms around me, and there's no stopping me. Each thrust, I go deeper. Each thrust, I'm moving her farther up the bed. I grab on to her hips, dragging her up onto my legs as I plunge in and out of her. She's gripping my arms, and I pull her up to sit on my lap. She straddles me, and with her breasts pressed to my chest, I hold on to her, raising my hips to meet hers. "Ride me, Lily. Take what you want from me. It's yours."

Her hips rotate front to back, side to side. She finds a rhythm and is relentless as she grinds on my lap. I'm so close. I reach between us and press my thumb to her clit, circling it until she's saying my name, over and over.

"Take it, Lily. Take it, baby."

Her pussy gets even hotter, and she starts to writhe as her juices coat my dick. She's coming, and as she spasms around me, I give up all control, shooting my cum deep inside her womb. Her body is trembling around me, and I cradle her in my arms, holding her to my chest.

When our breaths return to somewhat normal, I lay her back on the bed. I watch her and she watches me. There's so much I want to say, but I don't. Not because I don't want to. Fuck, I want to scream what I'm feeling, and I want everyone to know it. But I don't think she's ready for all that, and I can't risk pushing her away.

"I'll be right back."

I go to the bathroom and clean myself up. She follows in behind me, turning on the spray of the shower. Surprise doesn't even begin to cover it. She has her hand out, checking the temperature of the water, but her eyes are on me. Her appreciative gaze travels down my body and back up again.

"You care if I use your shower?"

I walk over to her, pressing my front to her back. I lean down, kissing the side of her neck, and already my dick starts to harden. "That depends. You going to let me join you?"

She steps into the shower and looks at me over her shoulder. "Sure, I mean, we should probably try to conserve water."

I follow behind her, wrapping my arms around her waist and pulling her against me. Everything about this just feels right, and I don't want it to end. I slide my hands around her, one arm around her waist and one across her chest.

She wiggles her ass against me, and I kiss her neck. "Don't tempt me, Lily. I want that ass too. I want all of you."

She sucks in a breath before turning around and sliding her hands around my neck. "I've never—"

She cuts herself off and bites on her lip almost nervously. I reach up, smoothing my finger across her lip. "It's okay, Lily. I'm happy with whatever you want to give me."

She lets out a breath of relief. I hold back my smile

because I don't want her to think I'm making fun of her. The truth is, I will be happy just holding her in my arms. She has no clue how badly I've wanted to be close to her and now that she's letting me hold her and feel her body against mine—fuck, it's perfect.

I slide my hand down her body, plucking her hard nipple between my thumb and forefinger before sliding it down her thin waist and palming her pussy. "Now let's get you clean because I want to dirty you up again."

She nods. "I like how you think, Ford."

I reach behind her, pouring soap into my hand. The fact that she's going to smell like me makes my heart beat in triple time. I run my hand down her body as she leans against me. I take my time with her, and by the time I'm done, I'm holding her up on shaky legs. Fuck, I'll never get enough of her.

LILIAN

I wake up, exhausted. There were morning meetings to close out the conference, but Ford said since he met with so many people the day before, we could skip it.

I should feel guilty. I never blow off work, but I'm too spent to feel anything but satisfied.

I roll onto my back, throwing my arm over my face to block out the sunlight.

Ford just shifts beside me, and once I'm settled, he wraps his leg around mine and puts his arm across my chest, cupping my breast.

I clench my eyes and try to regulate my breathing. I don't want him to know I'm awake. Not yet.

I know when we get back, everything is going to

have to go back to the way it was before. I am his assistant, and he's my boss.

But the longer I lie here, the more I know that I'm not ready for it to end just yet. I turn to my side, facing him.

His eyes are closed, and he looks so handsome. I can't take this for granted, not a minute of it.

Even though I see him every day, I try to commit it all to memory. The once black hair that is now mostly silver and white. The beard and how it felt against my thighs last night. The feel of his hand, big and possessive as he touched every inch of my body. The feel of his hard abs and how they flexed when he moved in and out of me.

He's touched me everywhere, and I want to repay the favor.

I turn to my stomach, and he shifts again but doesn't open his eyes. I hold my breath as I crawl down the bed, taking the blanket with me. I position myself between his legs, his cock standing hard between his thighs.

I wrap my hand around his girth, and his eyes fly open.

He's smiling at me as he bunches the pillow under his head and then rests his head on his arms. "Fuck, Lily. What a way to wake up."

His voice is thick, and I close my eyes, savoring the sound of it. The dirty talk, the things he said to me, the way he made me feel. I don't want to forget any of it.

I stroke him, gripping him tighter. My voice is soft as I try to explain to him. "I was thinking about it, and you had your mouth on every part of me last night. I didn't get the same honors."

His hips flex, raising off the bed a little. His hands go to the sheets, and he pulls at them in anticipation. I rub my finger along his tip, rubbing the precum along his length. "What do you think, Ford? Is it okay that I want to taste you? I want to feel you at the back of my throat, and I want you grunting MY name now."

"Yes, fuck, Lily. Make it quick, honey. I'm not going to last. Just thinking about your mouth on me has me ready to shoot my load."

"Tsk, tsk, tsk," I say, shaking my head. "No way. I want you to come in my mouth. I want to taste you this time."

He grunts, and more precum oozes from his tip. I smile at the control I have over him. "You want that, don't you, Ford? You want my mouth on you, don't you?"

"Yes," he hisses.

I stick my tongue out and run it from the root of

his hard cock to the very tip. He sucks in a deep breath and lets it out slowly.

I open my mouth, taking him in. Up and down, he moans as his hips shift to meet me.

I close my eyes, and he grunts, "No, look at me, Lily."

I open my eyes and watch him as I take him as far down my throat as I can. He's big, and I use my hand to help me.

He's close. His cock gets even harder, and his breaths are coming in big, heavy pants. I kick my leg over his and settle my bare pussy on his leg. My clit is throbbing, and pressing into his leg is the only relief I get.

He moves his leg as I ride it.

Every sense is heightened, and I'm on the verge of coming myself.

"I need inside you, Lily."

I look at him questioningly but don't stop bobbing on his dick.

He leans down, putting his hands under my arms and dragging me up his body, flipping me onto my back.

Just as fast, he's plowing into me, stroking my insides.

"Yes," I groan.

My pussy is in spasms, and an orgasm shoots through me, but he's relentless. Over and over he thrusts into me, saying the same words. "Mine. You're mine, Lily. All mine."

I completely come undone and writhe underneath him. "Yes, Ford. Yes."

He comes and then falls on top of me. I welcome the weight of him and wrap my legs around his waist to hold him to me.

He tries to lift himself up, but I tighten my hold. "No, please... stay for just a minute."

He lies down again, and for just a second, I let myself wonder what it would be like to be with him just like this, every morning.

When I loosen my hold on him, he climbs up the bed and lies next to me, even though he's still halfway on my body.

I hold on to his arms that are wrapped around me, wishing I never had to let go. I let out a regretful sigh. "We have to leave soon, don't we?"

He comes up on his elbow. "We have time to see the sights before we leave."

I shake my head and cuddle closer to him. "Nope. I'm good right here."

We lie in each other's arms, and eventually his breaths even out.

I lie here for the longest time, just being in his arms.

After he wakes up from his nap, we shower and have a late breakfast, and then make our way to the private jet that is waiting for us. Neither he nor I are saying much.

It's not until I'm settled in my seat that everything starts to catch up with me.

This is over... and we barely got started.

I don't regret last night or this morning, but I should have done more to protect my heart. How am I going to work day after day next to him, knowing he can never be mine? What is going to happen if I leave Tennessee, even just for a little while?

All these things are piling up in my head, and my heart starts to race.

Ford, being the man he is, thinks I'm anxious about the plane ride home.

He holds my hand and talks to me soothingly.

Eventually, I fake sleep as I try to distance myself from everything.

I'm quiet most of the plane ride home, and only when we have landed do I open my eyes.

At first glance, it's obvious that Ford knew I was fake sleeping.

The way he's looking at me makes me feel guilty.

He carries my suitcase to his waiting car. I should have driven myself to the airport, but hindsight is twenty-twenty.

"Are you okay?"

I nod my head and force a smile to my face. "Yes, I'm good. Just tired."

Images from last night flash through my mind, and he must know what I'm thinking because he smirks at me.

"Come to the park with me and Ollie. His soccer buddies are going to play ball, and the families are doing a cookout."

I would love to go. I really would, but I also know that I need to put some distance between us. "I think I need to go home. I need to check on Carrie and get ready for the work week."

He reaches across the console, resting his hand on my knee. "Come on. You can't leave me to the single moms."

His words hurt. Only because I know that it probably won't be long before he finds a woman that he wants to spend time with. How am I going to handle that?

I shake my head and look out the window. "No, I really should go home. I'm sure you can handle it."

I try not to be jealous thinking of the women that

are no doubt going to be bidding for his time. I don't have the right to be jealous. He's my boss, and I'm just his assistant. One lapse in judgment doesn't mean I have any kind of rights over him.

As we pull into the driveway, I jump out of the car before he can come around. My phone rings, and I've never been so happy to have a distraction. I take the bag from Ford and hold the phone up for him to see. "It's Carrie. Thank you for the weekend, Ford. I had a really good time."

Before he can say anything, I'm turning on my heel and making my way to the front door. I dig my keys out of my purse and let myself in, falling back into the door. I had rejected the phone call from Carrie, which is the first time I've ever done that. But I need just a few minutes to get my bearings before I talk to anyone.

FORD

I should not have let her out of my sight.

I texted her last night, just to check in, and for the first time since I'd met her, she didn't reply to my text.

This morning, I dropped Ollie off at school and pulled into the parking lot at work on two wheels. I'm practically panting as I make my way down the hallway to the corporate offices.

Beau stops me as I walk past his office. "Good trip?"

I nod. "Yeah, good. I'll fill you in later today. I'm late for a call."

He doesn't question me any further, and when I see Lily at her desk, I finally let out a breath of relief. I don't know what I was thinking. It's not like she would just quit on me, but there's something obviously on her mind by the way she's not looking up from her computer screen.

I lean down into her line of vision. "Lily."

She doesn't smile. Hell, her lips don't tip up at all. "Good morning, Ford. You have a ten o'clock this morning and then you're free until two this afternoon. I set your coffee in your office just a minute ago. Everything has been confirmed for Ollie's party on Sunday. I was able to get a private room, and food has been ordered. Is there anything else you need from me?"

My eyes light up at her choice of words. I want to tell her fuck, yeah, there's plenty I need from her, but instead I tell her with a clenched jaw, "Yes, can I see you in my office, please?"

She nods, grabbing her pad of paper and pencil off her desk before standing up. I walk down the hall to my office, and when she comes in, I shut it behind her. "What's going on?"

She shrugs. "Nothing... what do you mean?"

My jaw clenches in frustration. "Bullshit, nothing. What is going on, Lily? Talk to me."

She's looking everywhere but at me. "Vegas was great, but it was a mistake."

"Mistake?" I ask her incredulously. Of everything I thought she might say, I never expected that.

She nods patiently. "Yes, a mistake. You're my boss, Ford. I don't want to lose my job and—"

I throw my hands up. "What? You think if you don't want to sleep with me that I'll fire you? Let's get one thing straight. I need you here, Lily. Nothing you can say or do—or not do—will change that."

She paces across the room. "Listen to me, Ford. I don't think you'll fire me if I don't sleep with you. That's not what I was saying. My life is different now. We need to just call it like it is. We had a weekend of fun, and now we're back in the real world. I wasn't looking for anything more."

She obviously wants space, but I don't want to give it to her. I trail after her across the room. "What do you want, Lily? What is it YOU want?"

She doesn't answer me, so I press further. "You want to sleep around, is that it?"

She gives me an offended look. "No, I don't want to sleep around." I blow out a breath, my patience wearing thin, and she continues, "Since I was 18, everything I did was for Carrie. I told myself that I would live for myself now."

I point at her. She's standing with her arms crossed over her chest, and it's obvious she doesn't want to listen to anything I'm saying. "And what, Lily? What does that mean?"

She puts her hands on her hips. "Exactly what I said. I'm doing what I want, Ford. We had a fling, but because of circumstances, that's all it can ever be."

Speechless, my mouth falls open. I was ready to commit wholly and completely to her. Fuck, I would put a ring on her finger if I thought she was ready. I thought we had a connection this weekend. I thought that we were building a future. I've never been more wrong about anything in my life. Fuck, I had no idea that she thought we would make love and that would be it.

How the hell am I supposed to work next to her day after day, knowing what it's like to have her ride my dick, screaming my name but knowing I can't touch her?

"Fuck," I grunt with my hands on my hips. This is not going how I wanted it to, and right now, I'm afraid I'm going to say something that I will regret.

How the fuck do I even deal with this when all I want to do is bend her over the couch and take her? I want to feel her body unravel again. I want to hear my name on her lips in that husky tone that tells me she's so close to the edge her pussy starts to vibrate.

I turn my back to her and look out the window at the distillery. Fuck, I can't even focus on my job anymore.

"Fine, Lily. You can get back to work."

She doesn't move. It's like I can feel her indecision running through her head. I don't turn around and look at her. I can't. If I do, there's no holding me back. I'm already worried that I've pushed her too far.

She sighs behind me. Fuck, I hate this.

She gets as far as the door before I stop her. Without turning to look at her, I say her name. "Lily."

She stops and she's soft-spoken. "Yeah, Ford?"

"Don't even think about quitting. I wasn't lying to you. I won't let you leave me... leave here."

I would think that would make her happy, but it doesn't. Her voice sounds almost pained in her reply. "Okay, Ford. I understand."

It's only when I hear the click of the door shutting behind her that I let out the breath I was holding. *How the hell am I going to do this?* I was ready to make this more permanent, and she wants to end it. I walk over to my desk and fall into my chair. This may be a setback, but I'm not giving her up without a fight.

Lilian

Ever since I walked out of Ford's office earlier, I've had a pit in my stomach. It's like even though I knew I was doing the right thing, it doesn't feel good.

And Ford's attitude hasn't helped either.

He hasn't said anything, but I can see in every look that he's disappointed in me. I'm at the filing cabinet when he walks back in from lunch—well, what was supposed to be lunch—but he's dressed in shorts and a T-shirt. His hair is wet, his shirt sticking to him, and I try not to let my gaze travel, but he's hard to resist. My voice cracks as I ask him, "Did you have a good uh, lunch?"

He grunts in response. "I had to work off some steam at the gym."

I nod in understanding because I know that feeling. Just looking at him makes me feel like I could run a mile or two. "Did it work?"

His gaze travels down my body and back up again, and I feel it as if it's his hand on me instead of just his eyes. He frowns at me with a pained expression on his face. "Well, I thought it did, but obviously fuckin' not. I'm going to take a shower. Hold my calls."

I nod, and as he is about to walk away, he digs his phone out of the bag he's carrying. "I've had some RSVPs for Ollie's birthday. Can you work on those for me?"

I grab the phone he's handing me, making sure not to touch his outstretched hand. He knows what I'm doing—or trying not to do—and gives me a knowing smirk.

I take his phone and sit down at my desk. I take three deep breaths before opening the messaging app. He wasn't kidding. I keep scrolling, seeing all the new unopened messages. I pull up the invite list on my computer and start making my way through the list. The further I get, the more I'm wanting to toss his phone in the wastebasket in the corner.

Message after message of women RSVPing that their son or daughter will be at the party and they are looking forward to seeing Ford. They are filled with heart emojis, and one even has a blowing kiss emoji.

I try to ignore it and tell myself I have no right to be jealous, but when a new message pops up, I have no choice but to read it. Ford won't care. Heck, he'd expect me to. He's given me free rein over his phone plenty of times. The message is from Nancy Tazewell. She's the mom of Ollie's best friend. She was also married until earlier this year. I punch my finger onto the message to open it and read.

> The party sounds great and Tommy and I will be there. Maybe the four of us can get together the night before. How about a playdate? The boys can play and you and I can catch up over a bottle of wine. Let me know. I'll make your favorite. 😉

And of course there is a winky face emoji glaring at me at the end.

I drop the offending phone and huff. The audacity. I mean really—responding to a six-year-old's birthday party invite is not the best time to try and get a booty call.

I'm still stewing fifteen minutes later when Isabella walks in. "Hey, Lilian! How's it going?"

I sigh in frustration. I want to talk to someone, but

it can't be Isabella. She's a good friend, but she's also Ford's sister-in-law. Heck, it's not a good idea for anyone here at work to know what happened between us. Before I can answer her, she looks at me worriedly. "What's wrong? Is Lucas working you too hard? I know he's trying to find a replacement for you-know-who."

Normally I would laugh. It's funny that no one mentions Lucas' ex-assistant's name. Not since the day she was let go after trying to mess with her and Lucas' marriage.

I shake my head. "No, Lucas is fine. It's Ford that is driving me crazy. I'm thinking about seeing if I can just move over to work for Lucas and let Ford find himself a new assistant."

I'm only half joking. I actually thought about it last night. If Ford starts seeing someone, could I still work for him? Maybe I should talk to Ford about working for Lucas instead.

Ford sticks his head out his office door. "I heard that, Lilian, and you can forget that happening. You're mine."

Issi's eyes about pop out of her head as she looks at her brother-in-law and then at me. The possessive tone in his voice has me twitching in my seat. I swear it's like he's claiming me just by that look he's giving me.

To cover up my heated cheeks, I roll my eyes. "Sure, 'cause you're the boss of me..."

Ford stands to his full height. "I am your boss."

Issi looks between Ford and me with a curious expression on her face. Ford throws his hand out, pointing to his door. "Lilian, can I see you in my office please?"

I look down at my desk, shuffling through papers and trying to act like I don't hear him.

His voice is even more demanding the second time around. "Lilian. In my office... please."

I huff a breath, put my hands on my desk, and push myself up. Grabbing his phone, I mutter to him. "Sure, BOSS. I'll be right there."

Issi is watching us closely, smiling. I almost forgot she was standing here. "You here to see Lucas? He's on a phone call, but you know he's told me to never make you wait. You can go on in."

"Thanks," she tells me.

I walk past Ford without looking at him. He shuts the door behind us, and I swear I hear him lock it.

"You're mine, Lily."

He says it gruffly, his voice filled with possessiveness, and my whole body reacts to it. My nipples pucker, and there's a throb in my lower belly that only one thing—one man—can cure.

I turn, ready to deny him, but the look on his face is full of seriousness. "Is this because of Ollie?" I blink in confusion, and he continues. "Are you distancing yourself from me because I have a son?"

I gasp. "I love Ollie. You know I do. Heck, Ford, that's crazy talk. Ollie is a plus for you, what are you thinking?"

He lets out a breath, and his shoulders drop. "So it's me. I'm the reason you don't want to be with me."

I blow out a breath, not prepared for this conversation in any way. "Ask me how many people I've had sex with."

He grimaces, and his hands fist at his sides. "I don't want to hear about you with another man."

I hold my fingers up. "Three. One was when I was 19. One when I was twenty-five, and well, you know the third one." I take a step toward him, still clutching his phone in my hand. "Ask me how many vacations I've been on? How many times I've done something that was just for me?"

He tilts his head. "How many?"

"None. Never. My whole life I've committed to doing the right thing—the responsible thing. I told myself that I was going to do things different now."

He reaches for me and then at the last second drops his hands. "So what? That's all this weekend was to you? You wanted to do something forbidden and irresponsible so you slept with your boss?"

The way he says it does make it seem forbidden, but why does it feel so right?

"Listen, I think this is going to hurt Ollie, and that's the last thing I want to do. Plus, I don't know what's going to happen. If Carrie moves to Georgia..." My voice trails off because I can't bring myself to say it.

"What? You'll leave?"

I shrug. I've thought about it, and I don't want to leave Whiskey Run. I don't want to leave Ollie and Ford either. And that right there scares the hell out of me.

"If she asked me to, I would go and help her get settled—make sure she's okay. I know she's my sister but—"

He cuts me off. "She's like a daughter to you—I understand."

I continue. "And here at the office... do you think I want to be known as the woman that sleeps with the boss?" I raise his phone and toss it to his desk. I'm getting way into my feelings now, and I need to be mad at him. "I replied to the RSVPs. You had a play date invite from Tommy's mom. Something about dinner and a bottle of wine. She's making your favorite."

I'm pointing at the phone like it's the problem. It's

not. I know it's not. I'm just mad—and jealous—and I don't know what to do with those feelings. "I'm going back to work."

He grabs on to my wrist when I try to walk by. "I'm not going to dinner with her. I'm not sharing a bottle of wine with her, and I'm not eating her food, even if she does make my favorite meal. The only person I want to do those things with are you."

I shake my head. I want this. I want this so badly with him, but I can't go for it. I don't have a choice right now. He pulls me to the edge of his desk and then sits down in his chair. His hands are at my waist and his grip on me is tight.

He's a man that is always in control, but right now, he looks lost. He scrunches up his nose, not liking the words that are coming out of his mouth. "So what? You want to keep this quiet? Just between us?"

FORD

She's jealous. That much is obvious by the way she's mad about Tommy's mom. And she's tempted to take me up on my offer. I can see in her face that she wants to.

Fuck, I don't want to hide any of this. I want the world to know that she's mine, and I belong to her, but if this is what she needs right now, I'll do it. Because she looks tempted.

She looks up at me through her long lashes. "You'd be okay with that? With not telling anyone about us?"

Fuck, I hate it actually, but that's not what I tell her. "I don't like it, but I'll take you any way I can have you."

"So we keep this between us? No one has to know?"

She looks almost hopeful. I don't like it, but I tighten my hands at her waist because I don't want the alternative. "Is that what you want? You want to keep this between us?"

She nods.

I lean forward, pressing my head to her belly. Fuck, I can't mess this up. My voice is hoarse when I lean my head back and ask her, "Are you going to go on dates with other men?"

She shrugs. "I'm not looking for anything serious. I can't."

This is ridiculous. She's crazy if she thinks I'll stand by while she dates another man. I slide my hand up her thigh, under her skirt and press my thumb to her clit. "And sex? You going to let another man touch you? Kiss you?"

Her head falls back, and she pushes her hips toward me. Her clit is swollen and her panties soaked. I reach up and pull them down her legs, letting them fall to her feet. I slide her skirt up to her waist so I can see her.

I lean in, letting her feel my breath against her core. Her hips flex in reaction because she wants my mouth on her. I press my tongue to her core, and she moans. I pull back and look up at her. "You think I'm going to let another man near you?"

"Ford—" she starts, but I don't let her finish.

My finger replaces my tongue, and I swirl it around her swollen nub. Her hips rock while her head falls back and she pushes herself toward me.

I pull my hand away and I see the brief panic on her face. She grabs on to me, not letting me get far. When her eyes are on mine, I tell her exactly what I'm thinking. "I don't share, Lilian. If I'm tasting this, no one else is."

"Ford," she whines, but I shake my head. I'm not giving in on this.

"I mean it, Lily. If we do this, you're not dating, you're not sleeping with anyone else. Just me. I'm the man you come to when you need something. You got it?"

She nods, but I don't relent. Not yet.

I slide my finger through her wet slit and pump my finger in and out of her. "Tell me, Lily. I need to hear you say it. Say you're mine."

I barely get the words out then I kiss her clit. Her hand goes to my hair, and she's holding me to her. "I'm yours, Ford. All yours."

I feast on her with a vengeance. It's been a little over twenty-four hours since I've touched her, and I don't want to wait another minute to have her coming undone in my arms.

I lift up to push her back on my desk, and her legs fall open.

"Oh, honey, how could you even think about keeping this from me?"

I slide my hands up her thighs, and she's mewling. "Ford, please... I need you."

My hips jerk at the needy tone in her voice. "You want my lips or my cock, Lily?"

She reaches for me. "Both, Ford. I need both."

I pull at the buttons of my dress pants and shove them down my thighs. My cock springs free already hard and ready to fill her.

I hold on to her, pulling her to the edge of the desk before positioning myself at her entrance. I'm only a few inches in when I press my lips to hers. I'm more forceful than I should be, but I don't want her to doubt in any way exactly who she belongs to.

I kiss her like there's no tomorrow, holding on to her neck as I violate her lips.

Her heels dig into my ass, but I don't care. It hurts, but it hurts good.

I reach down between us, applying pressure to her clit. I need to come. I need to coat her insides with my cum, but I can't do that. Not until she's satisfied.

I pull my lips from hers. "Come for me, Lily. I need you to come, baby."

She digs her nails into my arms, her whole body flexing as her orgasm shoots through her. I follow as her pussy spasms around me, taking me over the edge. "Yes." I groan as I plow into her.

Over and over until I've completely marked her.

Both of us are breathing heavily. Her lips are red and bruised, and her eyes are wide. I see the question in her eyes, and I'm thinking the same thing. *Did that really just happen? Did I really just fuck her on my desk at work?*

I did, and I have no regrets. Not one.

She's panting with her hand against my chest. I pull out and damn she looks good with my cum oozing out of her.

"We can't do that again."

My eyes fly to hers. I'm on the verge of flipping her over and spanking her ass right where she is when her hand fists in my shirt. "I mean, at work. From now on, we need to keep this out of the office."

I let out a breath, circling my hand around her neck. "Fine. But anywhere else, you're mine."

She shakes her head. "No, Ford. Not anywhere else. I won't have Ollie hurt over this. We need to play it cool. We're coworkers... friends, but that's it."

I lean my forehead to hers. I want to argue with

her. I want to make her see that she and I are perfect for each other, but she's not going to listen.

Her hand comes up to cup my jaw. "Ford, promise me you're all right with this."

"No dating other men," I grunt at her.

I'm not happy about this. Not one fucking bit.

LILIAN

He just made me come harder than I ever have in my life, but he doesn't look happy. If anything, he looks pissed off. "Fine. If I'm not dating any other man, then you're not drinking wine with Tommy's mom or dating other women."

He shrugs. "I told you in Vegas. I haven't even looked at another woman in two years. The only woman I want has her cum on my dick right now, so there's that."

I push him off me. "You're so crude, Ford."

He helps me off the desk, pulling my underwear up my thighs. I'm a mess, but he doesn't seem to care. He pats my panty-clad pussy before bringing my skirt down to cover my hips. "It's not crude when it's the truth."

He points at his manhood, and sure enough, it's shiny from our release. I watch as he stuffs himself in his underwear and pulls his pants up. I'm biting on my lip when he completely covers himself from me.

"What? Were you not finished? I can put off my afternoon meetings."

Licking my lips, I put some distance between us as I try to finger-brush my hair. I can feel that my lips are swollen, my body is aching and I'm sure it shows exactly what we've been doing in here. "How do I look?"

He smirks at me, obviously proud of himself. "You look satisfied."

I tap my foot on the floor and roll my eyes. "That's not what I meant but yeah, I am satisfied. I'm going to use your restroom to freshen up before I go back out there."

He comes over and kisses me until I'm breathless. "Good idea. I'm going to a meeting—"

I point down at his nether regions. "You don't think you should clean up a little before you go?"

He leans down and whispers in my ear, "Nope. I like having you on me." He kisses my neck and is out the door before I can respond. In one fell swoop, I fall against the door he just walked out of.

I just gave in to my boss.

I want everything that Ford has to offer, but I'm scared. What if I'm not enough? What if he changes his mind?

I told myself that I was going to chase my dreams and do what I want, but does that mean I can't be with Ford too?

What if my sister leaves? Can I tell her no, that I won't go with her after I've promised her that I will always be there for her when she needs me?

The satisfaction I was feeling only moments ago is fleeting, and now all I feel is turmoil. I make my way to the bathroom and look at myself in the mirror. I'm a mess. I run my fingers through my hair, clean myself up, and then walk back out into Ford's office. I straighten up his desk and notice he's left his phone. I give it a dirty look because I'm thinking about the text from Tommy's mom that has gone unanswered.

I barely make it out to my desk and Beau is standing in the hallway. "Hey. Have you seen Lucas or Ford?"

I point at Lucas' door. "Lucas was in his office with Isabella a while ago. I'm not sure if they're still in there.

Ford had a meeting in town but should be back shortly. Can I help you with something?"

He's shaking his head. "No, I was just wanting to check in with them. I'm sorry about what happened with Jim Ogle while you were in Vegas."

I hold my hand up. "Please, I'm the one that's sorry that you lost his business."

He shakes his head. "We don't want his business."

I nod quickly to change the subject and ask about his wife. "How's Natalie? I haven't seen her in a while."

Pain is reflected in his eyes, but he forces a smile to his face. "She's fine. She's okay. Uh, I'm going to go out to the plant and see if I can catch Austin. I'll see you later."

I nod and watch him walk away. I really should call and catch up with Natalie. Determined to do just that, I make my way to my desk, but before I can pick up the phone, a woman stops in front of my desk. She looks unsure and a little nervous. I give her my best smile. "Hello. May I help you?"

She nods, looking around at the office before looking at me again. "Hi. I'm Elle Grace. I saw the ad in the paper. I was hoping to apply for the assistant's job that is open."

I barely stop myself from jumping up and down. "Great. Do you have a resume?"

She nods and pulls a folder from her tote bag that is hanging over her arm. She seems unsure when she hands me the piece of paper. "I don't have a lot of experience. I can type ninety to a hundred words a minute. I'm a fast learner, I'm dependable, and I work hard."

I take the resume from her and scan it quickly. Her job history is limited to one previous position. But it says that she is skilled in all of the software that we use here. Honestly, she reminds me of myself when I first applied for a job at Blaze Whiskey.

"Do you care to wait in the conference room down the hall? I am going to see if Lucas is available to interview you."

I point to the half-opened door, and she goes to it, disappearing inside. I would want to hire someone with more experience, but for some reason, I can't let her leave.

I buzz into Lucas' office, and when he answers, I explain the situation.

"Give me five minutes. I'll be right there."

I grab two cups of coffee and make my way to the conference room. She's sitting with her hands on the table in front of her. "Thank you," she says, taking a sip of the warm liquid.

"Tell me about yourself. Why do you want to work here?"

She holds her hands together and says, "I just recently moved to Whiskey Run, and when I saw the ad, I thought I'd be a good fit. I have a lot of the requirements for the job. I worked in the office at a textile plant in Texas. Of course, we made clothes there, so entirely different thing, but I would assume a lot of the assistant work is the same. Like I said, I'm a quick learner."

Lucas comes in, adjusting his tie. His cheeks are ruddy as he walks into the room. "Hello. I'm Lucas Blaze. It's nice to meet you."

Elle sits back in her seat, her eyes wide. There's no mistaking the fear on her face, but just as quickly it disappears, and she reaches out her hand. "Hello. I'm Elle Grace. It's nice to meet you."

Lucas, as if understanding what's going on, moves so that I'm between him and Elle. "Well, Elle, tell me about yourself."

She repeats what she told me, but this time she does so even more nervously. Lucas is looking at the resume I slid to him, and when Elle stops talking, he glances up at her. "We require a background check. Is that a problem?"

She looks shocked and then uneasy. She pulls her bag up on her shoulder and stands up. "Unfortunately, that's not possible. I'm sorry for wasting your time. I should have realized that would be a requirement."

Lucas remains seated and holds his hands out, palms up. "It's okay. Sit down, please."

She is breathless as she sits down. She's sitting rigidly, looking as if she's about to run. Lucas and I exchange a look, and I see the decision on his face.

"It looks like you have all the qualifications. You would be working with Lilian here. She would be the one training you. May I ask you why a background check is out of the question?"

She's still holding tightly on to her bag. "Because I have someone in my past that I don't want to know where I am."

Lucas levels her with a stare before nodding his head. "You're hired. You can start on Monday."

Elle's mouth drops, and she stutters, "I'm, uh, hired?"

He nods, all business. "Yes. If you want the job."

She nods her head. "Yes. Yes, I want the job."

He smiles. "Good. It's yours. Lilian, can you please show her where HR is? You know what? After she's done filling out the paperwork, put it on my desk. I'll take care of it after she fills it out."

I nod happily. "Will do, boss."

"I'll see you next Monday, Ms. Grace," he says, but before he can get out the door, Elle stops him.

"I have to ask. Why are you doing this?"

He shrugs off the question, but she's right in asking it. To some people, this would be considered a problem hiring her. She sounds as if she's going through some things, and most businesses would not want to take her on knowing that. "You need a job, and Lilian needs some help around here. You can thank her for the job, though. If she didn't want to hire you, you wouldn't have made it in here past five minutes. She definitely wouldn't have brought you coffee."

I know he's thinking about the woman I escorted out the other day, but I don't care. Looking at Elle, I know she's going to be a good fit here.

"Come on, I'll show you around the place, and we can pick up the papers from Human Resources."

I show her around the plant and then take her to Human Resources to pick up a hiring packet. We go back to where her desk is, and I let her sit there to fill out everything. There's a thousand things I want to ask her, but I don't. I don't want to scare her off by being nosy.

It's almost time to leave when Ford comes back through the door. He stops in front of my desk, and the look he gives me has my whole body reacting. I point to the woman at the other desk. "Lucas hired an assistant. Elle, this is Ford Blaze. Ford, Elle. I'm his assistant," I explain to her.

She stares wide-eyed at him and gives him a timid wave. "Hello. It's nice to meet you."

He nods. "It's nice to meet you. Welcome aboard."

He turns back to me. "Ollie has practice tonight, so I'll be there. Do you need me for anything?"

Looking at him, I'm thinking of earlier, and I can feel my face turn red as I remember basically that I begged him to have sex with me. Hell, I promised him all kinds of things for it. "No, I'll call you if something comes up. Tell Ollie I'll see him Thursday for the cupcakes. I haven't forgotten."

He chuckles. "Ha, there's no way he'd let you forget that."

I nod and watch him disappear into his office. Elle is watching me with a curious glance on her face, but I just smile at her. "Well, I think we're all done here. You ready to call it a day?"

She nods and follows me out. I watch as she gets

into her small hatchback car and drives off. A part of me wants to go back inside where Ford is, but I don't. Instead, I drive home and try to put some distance between us. After one weekend of being with him, I've found that I miss him when I'm not with him. But that's my problem to deal with.

FORD

I'm sitting in Lilian's driveway hoping that I'm doing the right thing. I gather the bags from the passenger seat and make my way up the front steps of her porch. It's been two days of back-to-back meetings and then in the evenings I've been busy with Ollie. Finally, I'd had enough. I asked my brother Austin to watch Ollie, and I grabbed food from Red's Diner.

I ring the doorbell and wait.

Lily comes to the door and looks at me in surprise. "Ford? What are you doing here?"

She at least looks happy to see me. "Well, I thought we could have a date tonight." I hold up the bag of food.

She points at it and crosses her arms. "By any chance is there apple cinnamon Blaze cake in there?"

I nod knowingly. Red's Diner uses our branded cinnamon whiskey to make this cake, and it's award winning. "Of course. I knew I had a better chance of you letting me in if I brought it."

She reaches for the bag, and I jerk it away from her with a laugh. "Nice try. I'm not a fool. You letting me in?"

She moves to the side and waves for me to go in. "Come on."

I kiss her as I walk in. It's been too long since I've touched her, and that's the first thing I wanted to do.

I force myself to let go and move into her house. I lead us into the kitchen and start unloading the food I brought. I put the burgers and fries on the plates she brings to set on the counter.

"Mmmm," she says as she looks at the pile of the food.

"I was hoping you hadn't eaten yet."

She gives me a look full of lust and winks at me. "I'm starving, but you can help me with that later."

I grab on to her wrist before she picks up her plate. "I can help you with that now."

She doesn't seem unhappy about it so I lift her up and set it her on the counter. She shrieks and giggles as

I move between her legs. "Ford, we don't want our food to get cold."

I clench my hand on to her waist. "I don't need food. I need you."

She lifts a French fry off her plate and holds it to my lips. "Food. Real food, Ford. I need sustenance."

I wrap my hand around hers and put the fry in her mouth and then I lean in to kiss her neck. "You can have your dinner, and I'll have mine."

Her hands run up and down my chest, and she groans. "Ford, are you going to be mad if you have to eat a cold burger?"

I suckle her breast through her thin T-shirt. "Do I get to eat you instead?"

She lifts her shirt up, and I move back to let it pass. As soon as she has it off, I'm latched on to her. She pushes her hands through my hair, holding me to her breast. "I'm not going to tell you no."

I push her backwards, and she lifts her hips so I can shimmy her shorts down her legs. I've been here less than five minutes, and I already have her naked and ready for me. I feast on her as her moans fill the air.

I love hearing her cry out my name, and I drag it on, bringing her to the edge, letting up and then bringing her further the next time. She puts her hand at the back of my head, gripping my hair. "Please, Ford. I need to come."

I want her to know that I'll always give her what she wants. I suckle her clit, and her hips gyrate as her body is pulled taut in an orgasm. I don't let up, letting her ride it out until she's breathless and lying limply across the kitchen counter. I'm smiling when I tug her to sit up.

She looks at me through hooded eyes, and I lift a French fry to her lips. She takes it and chews slowly. She's watching me and she leans down, picking up the hamburger and holding it up to me. "We going to feed each other now?"

She blushes. "I figure it's the least I can do after that."

I laugh and take a bite of the food she's holding in my face. She sits naked on the counter, and we take turns feeding each other.

We eat most of our burgers and some of our fries before she looks down at herself. "I should probably get dressed."

I pull at the T-shirt in her hands. "Nah, I like you naked."

She pushes off the counter, confident in her own skin, grabs the two pieces of cake and two forks, and sashays away from me. "Want to lie in bed and eat cake?"

I follow behind her and watch as she sets the cake on the nightstand, pulls the cover back, and gets into bed. "You coming?"

I kick off my shoes and go to sit in her bed, but she holds her hand up. "Nope, you want in here, you have to be naked."

I laugh, loving this playful side of her. I take off my clothes, her eyes on me the whole time. My cock is hard and has been since I walked in the front door. She looks at me appreciatively, and I sit down on the bed next to her, trying my best to ignore the tent in the covers over my erection.

She points at it. "Maybe before the cake, I should take care of that for you."

I pull her to me, and she pushes down the sheet as she straddles my lap. I stare up at her, overcome by having her near. "It won't take long. I haven't been inside you in forty-eight hours."

She goes to her knees and wraps her hand around my girth, fitting me to her entrance. "Are we counting now?"

I nod, sucking in a breath as she impales herself on my length. "Yes, I count every minute that I'm not with you."

She looks at me curiously. She looks almost hopeful. I grab on to her hips, helping her grind against me. This may not be the time, but I can't help it. "This is something real, Lily."

She gives me a playful smirk as she bounces on my lap. "I'll give it to you. It's definitely something."

Frustration consumes me, and I act before thinking. I flip her onto her back and hover over her, my body pressed to hers. I hold my hand to the side of her face, forcing her to look up at me. "No, Lily. You can deny it all you want. You can try to convince yourself this is a fling and something that needs to be hidden, but the truth is... this thing between me and you... this is something real."

She blinks, and emotion clouds her face. "Ford?"

I position myself inside her and thrust slowly in and out. Our eyes are fixed on each other, and my heart is pounding in my chest. "This is something REAL."

"But—" she starts, and I shake my head, grunting. "No, don't make excuses... don't act like you don't want this. I don't want to take anything from you. I don't want you to push your dreams aside. I just want you to admit that this between us... it's real, Lily."

I lift her hips up and hit her at a different angle. Her face scrunches up, but her eyes never leave mine.

I put my hand at her pussy, circling her clit with my thumb. "Say it, Lily. I need to hear you say it."

She's so close. Her whole body is vibrating underneath me as her hips jerk. "It's real, Ford. I know it is. It's REAL!" she shouts as she topples into ecstasy. I come with her. I have no choice when she's clamped onto me like a vise.

Our breathing is hectic, and I lean over her, watching her closely. Her expression is unguarded, and I want to tell her how I feel. I want her to know that I love her and I won't be letting her go, but already, just with her confession, I can see she's freaked out a bit. I press my lips to hers and pull back before lying down beside her.

We're both quiet as we get cleaned up and then we lie back down in her bed. She has her T-shirt back on, and I'm in my underwear while we eat cake.

"What are your dreams, Lily? What do you want to do?"

She seems taken aback but recovers quickly. "I loved photography. That's what I wanted to do."

She looks at some portraits on the wall, and I notice them for the first time. I get out of bed and make my way across the room. "Did you take these?"

She nods, and I stare at the images. They are so beautiful. She's captured sunsets, mountains, lakes, and flowing rivers, and each one looks almost magical. I point at the sunset. "How did I not know this about you?"

She shrugs. "It's a hobby. All of those are taken here in Whiskey Run. I had to have a real job, and even though I wanted to travel and study the art of photography, I couldn't."

I stand with my back to her, looking at each of the images. They are not just point and shoot pictures. They each have emotion in them. "You missed your calling, Lily. Don't get me wrong, you're a great assistant. The best. But these... they should be hung in galleries, not in your room for no one to see."

The mood in the room is palpable, and I turn to look at her. "Does Carrie know that you wanted to be a photographer? Does she know how good you are?"

She rolls her eyes. "She's my sister. I could draw a stick figure and she'd think it was good. But yeah, she knows I wanted to be a photographer. Trust me, she's bothered by it. She thinks I gave it all up for her, and I've tried to explain to her that it's not her fault. I wouldn't have wanted to travel and see the world. I wanted to be here for her."

I recall what she told me in Vegas about her nightmares and the way she would cling to Lily. "You had to."

She plays it off like it's not a big deal. "I wanted to. And I think that's why she's on me now. She wants me to go for all the things she thought I gave up on."

I walk over to her and sit next to her. "What about you? She worked through it in therapy, and she had you to help her. Who helped you?"

She lies back, putting her arms under her head as she stares at the ceiling. "I went to therapy a few times. I'm scared of falling in love. I know what it's like to lose someone you love, and I have a hard time putting myself in a position to go through that again. And there's parts of me that think I'll never be good enough."

I put one hand on each side of her head and lean over her. "You're more than enough, Lily."

She brings her hands from under her head and puts them on my chest. She plays with the patch of hair there, running her fingers through it. "You think I'm enough?"

Fuck, how could she not know? "Yeah, baby, enough doesn't even cut it. You're everything."

At this moment, I know I can give her everything she wants. I can encourage her to reach for her dreams. I can help her with all of it. I can easily get a professional camera, I can set her up with the biggest photographer in New York, I can get her space in a gallery show. I can do all of it with just a few phone calls. But if I do all that and help her reach her dreams, will I end up losing her in the process?

I kiss her then, sealing my mouth over hers. It's either that or I tell her that I love her and I can't lose her—neither of which I think she wants to hear.

LILIAN

I'm addicted to Ford Blaze.

What we had in Vegas was fun and earth-shattering, but now what's happening between us is soul-shattering. He has me questioning everything I thought I wanted, every dream I've had, and what my future looks like.

So much so, I've been putting off my call to Carrie.

I stare at the phone and know that I need to call her.

My body is still tingling from my time with Ford earlier. He had to leave to go pick up Ollie from Austin's house, and now here I sit, staring at my phone, knowing I need to make the call. I dial Carrie's number and put the phone to my ear.

"Hey, sis!" she answers.

"Hey Carrie Bear. How's it going?"

She bursts out laughing. "Carrie Bear? Really? I'm not five anymore."

I lie back on the couch. "I know, but you'll always be my little Carrie Bear."

"How was your Vegas trip?" she asks at the same time I ask her, "How was your honeymoon?"

"You go first! I want to hear about the honeymoon."

I close my eyes and listen to her. Not only what she's saying but the pure happiness in her voice. There was a time that I wondered if she'd ever fully recover from our loss. And by no means has she forgotten it, but at least it's bearable now.

"I'm so happy for you, Carrie." I try to hide the emotion in my voice. "I can't wait to see the wedding pictures. You were the most beautiful bride I've ever seen."

Before she can ask me about Vegas—because at this point, I'm not ready to talk about it, not yet—I ask, "Has Phillip heard anything about his promotion?"

She blows out a breath. "He's putting off answering them. More money is tempting, but we just don't know. I'm supposed to start the teaching job at the elementary school next semester, but if it comes down to it, I can teach anywhere. I just don't know, sis.

I don't want to hold him back because I know this can be huge for him, but neither one of us really want to leave Whiskey Run. Our family, our friends are all here. I can't leave you, Lily. I can't."

The happiness from her voice earlier is gone now, and I wish I hadn't brought it up. "Don't worry, sis. We'll figure it out. You and Philip need to make a decision on what's best for you. Don't think about anyone or anything else."

"But you..." she starts.

I clench my eyes shut. Before I would have promised her the world without even thinking. I can still promise it to her, but it causes a pain in my chest when I say it. "I've told you all along, Carrie. I will always be here for you. Always. If you need me... I'm there."

Carrie sighs loudly into the phone. "Thank you, sis. I don't know what I would do without you."

"I love you too," I tell her. We talk for a few minutes until Philip gets home. I'm glad that she didn't ask me about Vegas or my trip with Ford again. I'm not ready to talk about it. Probably because I'm not ready to admit just how much he's come to mean to me. Everything is up in the air and uncertain. Now is not a good time to be falling in love.

FORD

I sit out of the way at the counter in my kitchen.

Ollie and Lily don't need me. Heck, there's a hundred other things I could be doing, but nothing could drag me out of this room right now.

Lily showed up right on time, her arms weighed down with grocery bags. I gave her the recipe for Granny's icing earlier today, and it looks like she took this whole cupcake baking thing to heart.

The laughter between Ollie and Lily is heartwarming to hear. They are both smiling ear to ear as they work, and even though I want to jump in and be a part of it, Ollie needs this, and so I sit here and watch them.

Lily just finished making the icing, and she gets a

spoon out of the drawer, puts a heaping of the icing on it, and holds it up to Ollie. "You have to try it. If it's not right, just tell me, and we can try it again."

She looks worried as Ollie takes the spoon and looks at it. He's taking her request to heart and makes a big deal of smelling it and then taking a small lick of it.

I swear Lily is holding her breath until Ollie's eyes light up. "It's perfect. Oh Lily, it tastes just like Granny's."

He no sooner sets the spoon down then he bursts into tears. Lily's eyes get as wide as saucers as Ollie dives off the chair he's standing on and flings himself into her arms. She catches him and holds on to him as he sobs against her chest.

I'm out of my chair and across the room in an instant. "Ollie, you okay, buddy?"

He starts to sniff. Lily is rubbing his back, cooing to him that everything is okay.

Finally, when he starts to calm down, he lifts his head, sniffing. "I know I shouldn't cry, Dad—"

Lily lifts him up higher on her waist. She's a tiny thing, and I know he's too big for her to hold, but when I try to take him, she holds him tighter. She sets him up on the counter and stands in front of him. "It's okay to cry, Ollie. Are you missing your granny?"

He nods as Lily wipes his eyes and then his nose. "Do you know that even now, I cry when I'm missing my mom and dad?"

Ollie's eyes go round. "You do?"

Lily nods and looks over at me. "Do you know that your dad is sad sometimes and misses Granny? He cries too, Ollie."

Ollie doesn't believe her and looks at me. "No way. Do you, Dad?"

I nod and walk closer to them, putting one hand on Ollie's back and the other on Lily's back. "Yeah, I do, son. I miss Granny too. But you know what helps me when I miss her?"

He shakes his head. "No, what?"

"Talking about her. Looking at pictures of her. Baking cupcakes that she always liked to make for you. That's how we can keep her with us, Oll. That's how we can remember her. She loved you so much, and I'm sure she's looking down on you right now, wishing she could hug you and tell you that everything's going to be okay."

He looks at Lily. "You believe that, Lily?"

She nods instantly. "Oh, definitely. There's no doubt about it. I'd say she's happy that you wanted to continue the tradition of making cupcakes for your birthday. And she'll be happy tomorrow to know that your dad is bringing them to your school party."

He nods, wiping his nose on his sleeve. Now's not the time to get on him about hygiene, so I let it go. "That's right, buddy. And from now on, any time you feel sad or you want to talk about Granny, we can. I know Uncle Lucas, Beau, Huddy, and Austin would love to too. Anytime you want to talk about Granny, I'll listen, okay?"

"Okay."

I run my hand through Ollie's hair. "We have to let the cupcakes cool before we ice them. What do you think about going to get that present we got for Lily?"

His eyes light up. "I thought we had to wait."

I shake my head. "Nope. I think we should give it to her now."

"No, you guys shouldn't have gotten me anything. It's Ollie's birthday."

Ollie jumps off the counter, and I help him to the ground. He runs out of the room and is back, holding a big, wrapped box, his face happy again.

I lean over to Lily. "Look at that face. Can you really tell him no?"

She swats at me and then wipes at her own wet eyes. "You know I can't."

I walk with her over to the table and hold the seat

out for her. Ollie puts the box in front of her and claps his hands together. "Open it. Open it. Dad said you're going to love it."

She has her hands on the box and looks at Ollie. "You could draw me a picture, and I'd love it, Ollie. I don't need you and your dad to buy me gifts."

Ollie barks out a laugh. "Dad said you'd say that, but he thought this would make you really happy. Please open it, Lily."

She laughs and musses his hair. "Okay, you win. I'll open it."

She takes her time removing the wrapping paper, and when she sees the box, her mouth drops. "Ford... what did you do?"

She's quicker to open it, and when she gets the box open, she takes out the professional grade camera and looks at it in awe. "Ford," she admonishes, shaking her head.

I reach over and wrap my hand around her forearm. I can see how much this gift means to her, "I want you to have it. Ollie and I wanted to get something for you because you're so special to us."

What was meant to soothe her actually has the opposite effect. She starts to sob, and Ollie goes to hug her. "Don't cry, Lily."

She sniffs and looks at him. "I'm crying because

I'm happy. This is the best gift anyone had ever given me. Thank you, Ollie." She lifts her eyes to mine. "Thank you, Ford. I love… it."

For just a second there, I thought she was going to say she loves me. I felt my heart expand in my chest and just as quickly, it dropped. "You're welcome. I know you want to try it out. You want me and Ollie to finish the cupcakes?"

She shakes her head. "No way. I've heard all about you burning water. How is that even possible? But yeah, I'd like for you to kindly stay away from the cupcakes."

I hold my hands up with a laugh. "Fine. No problem."

She carefully sets the camera back in the box, and she and Ollie go back to the counter. I sit and watch as they ice the cupcakes, and when they're all done, she goes over to the bags she brought with her. "All right, Ollie. One more thing and then we'll be done."

He shakes his head. "They look perfect, Lily. What are they missing?"

She grabs something from the bag, holds it behind her back, and walks back over to him. She brings it around with a flourish. "These!"

He gets excited, jumping up and down in the chair he's standing on. She hooks one arm around his waist so he doesn't fall and laughs with him. "I saw these soccer balls and I thought these would look perfect on the top of your cupcakes. I mean, since you're such a good soccer player, you need to have soccer balls on your cupcakes, right?"

He's nodding his head as she opens the package. They put a soccer ball on the top of each cupcake, and then I help them pack it all in the carrying tray that she brought with her.

I pat Ollie on the back. "Tell Lily thank you and go on up to get ready for bed."

He turns to Lily. "Will you come to my party?"

She nods her head. "Sunday? You know I wouldn't miss it."

He shakes his head and looks at her almost bashfully. "No, my birthday party at school tomorrow. The other kids have their moms come and hand out cupcakes and sing happy birthday to them."

I wait for Lily to freak out. This is exactly what she was wanting to avoid, but there's no escaping it now. My son is already attached to her. I'm sure it happened all those times when Granny was sick and I needed to be with her. Lily took him to school, picked him up, and came to his games—she's done everything for him, and obviously it's meant a lot to him.

She puts her hand to her chest. "Yes, of course I'll be there. What time is it?"

He shrugs and rolls his eyes. "Right after lunch. They make us eat our food first."

She laughs at that. "I'll talk to my boss, but I think I can work it out."

Ollie laughs and looks at me. "Isn't Daddy your boss?"

She nods and looks up at me. "Yes."

Ollie pleads with me. "Please, Daddy, can Lily bring cupcakes with you? Please?"

I see Lily nod her head at me, and I tell Ollie, "Yes. Of course. Now time to get ready for bed. I'll be up in a little while to tuck you in."

Ollie is pounding his fist into the air with excitement and then comes to hug me and then Lily before running out of the room. "Thanks for making cupcakes with me, Lily."

She calls after him, "You're welcome!"

Instantly, I turn to Lily, and the smile has dropped off her face. She's going to get her stuff together and finish cleaning up, and I follow behind her. "Don't freak out on me, Lily."

She's wiping down the already clean counter. "This is what we needed to avoid, Ford. I don't want to let him down. I can't let him down."

"It's just tomorrow you promised him. You can go tomorrow. It's going to be okay, just breathe."

She takes to heart what I said and takes a deep breath. "I'm honored, I really am, Ford. I love that kid, but I don't want to hurt him. How is he going to handle it if I have to leave? What then?"

I freeze up at her words. "What are you not telling me, Lily? Is Carrie…"

My voice trails off when she shakes her head. "No, I mean, nothing has been decided. Philip is putting off his company, and they are weighing their decision. Carrie did say that if they go, she wants me there, but I'm not going to worry about it until the time comes."

She's lying to me. I can tell by the way her forehead is creased and the look in her eye that she's worried about it. I pull her into my arms, and thankfully she doesn't resist me. "One day at a time, Lily. We're going to take it one day at a time."

She wraps her arms around me and rests her chin on my chest to look up at me. "That camera is too much."

I brush a strand of hair off her face and kiss her forehead. "Nothing is too much for you. I wanted you to have it. I believe in you and your dreams, Lily."

She sighs and rests her cheek against me. "Oh Ford, what are we going to do?"

I rest my cheek on the top of her head. "We're going to make this work, Lily. I told you once and I'll say it again. I'm not letting you go."

She doesn't say it, but I know what she's thinking. I may not have a choice but to let her go.

Lilian

I'm pulling into the parking lot at school the next day, and my phone dings, alerting me to a new message. I turn off the car and grab it, opening the messaging app as I walk around to grab the boxes of cupcakes. I can't be late for this, but seeing my sister's name, I know I need to at least read it. I tense as I read her message.

Come over tonight. We're celebrating Philip's new job.

My heart literally drops in my chest, and I suck in a horrified breath. *It's happening.*

Emotion hits me hard. I thought I was successful in keeping my wall up and my heart guarded, but obviously not because right now I feel like curling into the fetal position and crying my eyes out. I don't respond to her texts. I can't right now because I have to go in and make a little boy's birthday party the best he's ever had.

I toss my phone onto the floorboard, put my new camera over my shoulder, grab the bags of things I picked up from the store, and then juggle the boxes of cupcakes in my hand. It would be nice to have another set of hands, but Ford had an emergency meeting all morning, and we had to drive here separately. Luckily, I spot his car a few aisles down and I know he's at least inside.

I get to the office, and they buzz me through.

I walk down the hall and into Ollie's homeroom and force a smile to my face, acting as if I don't have a care in the world except this little boy's birthday party. As soon as Ollie sees me, he's up out of his seat, sprinting to me. "Lily, you made it!"

I throw my head back with a big laugh. "Of course I made it, but I had to stop and get a few things too. Mrs. Jackson, is it okay if Ollie helps me pass everything out?"

She nods and waves her approval, not paying me or the kids a bit of attention. It seems that she has Ford cornered. He really does catch the eye of all women. Mrs. Jackson is at least sixty years old, but the way she's flirting with him while patting her hair says she's interested.

I hand the plates and napkins to Ollie, and he goes around the room, passing them out. I follow behind him handing out party hats, which Ollie gets a big kick out of. As soon as everyone has their party gear, we go around handing out cupcakes. When everyone has one, I take pity on Ford and wave him over. "We're going to sing to the birthday boy now!"

Ford walks away from Mrs. Jackson and stops behind me, putting his hands on my shoulders. Half the kids have already stuffed the cupcakes in their mouths, but it doesn't matter. I pick up my camera, ready to capture it all.

Ollie is standing at the front of the classroom, and I lead the class in singing happy birthday. He's smiling from ear to ear, looking around at everyone. He's happy, and I'm so glad that I could be here for it. I walk around the room taking pictures of Ollie with his friends. I want to capture all of it.

I'm taking pictures of Ford and Ollie when Mrs. Jackson comes over to stand next to me. "You must be Lilian. Ollie talks about you all the time."

"I am, Mrs. Jackson, and likewise, Ollie talks about you all the time too." I smile at her even though Ollie's usually complaining about too much homework or how his teacher was too tired to have outdoor recess today. But she doesn't need to know that.

She nods and pats my hand. "He's a special little boy. I'm so glad he has you in his life. A boy needs a mother, that's for sure."

I shake my head. "Oh, I'm not, I mean, I'm sure he's told you that I'm not his mother."

She seems amused. "Well, honey, you may not be his biological mother, but you're the very definition of the word. You love that little boy, and he loves you. That's all that matters."

She pats me once more before going over to break up a squabble on the other side of the room. I let her words sink in and wait for panic to hit me, but it doesn't. I look at Ollie laughing with his friends, and his dad is watching me closely. It's like he's waiting for me to freak out. I give him a reassuring look. He sighs and gives me a flirty smile. I can't help but lift the camera in my hands and take his picture.

He's smirking with a glint in his eye the whole way over to me. *How am I going to walk away from him? How can I?*

Just the thought makes me sick to my stomach, and I have to look away from him. I try to focus on the kids around us instead of the decision I'm going to have to make soon.

Ford stops next to me and touches my shoulder. "You okay?"

I nod and hide myself behind the camera. I take some more pictures, but I can feel Ford's gaze on me.

"All right, who wants to play a game?" I call out to the class because I need to put some distance between Ford and me.

The whole class hollers yeah, and I move to the front of the classroom. "Okay, does everyone know how to play Simon Says?" It's a game I played in school when I was little. Hopefully, these kids have played it at one time or another.

A few hands go up, and I quickly explain the rules of the game. For the next thirty minutes, I lead the class in Simon Says. When Mrs. Jackson announces that it's time for them to start math class, I take it that it's our time to leave.

Ford and I are cleaning up the leftover cupcakes and getting ready to leave when Ollie runs up to us, giving us each a hug. He has icing on his mouth, and I'm pretty sure he snuck a second cupcake. He smears it on my shirt as he hugs me. "I love you, Lily."

I squeeze him tightly, close my eyes, and breathe him in. "I love you too, Ollie."

He fist-bumps his dad, tells him he loves him, and joins the rest of the class.

Ford takes some of the things out of my hands until I'm only carrying my camera. I hold it up as we're walking out of the school. "I love my present."

He nods. "I'm glad. I can't wait to see the pictures. Thank you for being here today, Lily. I know it wasn't easy for you, but I want you to know it meant the world to Ollie... and to me."

A flash of grief hits me hard and quickly. I choke back a sob. "Uh, do you care if I take the rest of the day off?"

He shakes his head. "Of course not. Do you have plans? Because if not, I'd love for you to come over to dinner tonight."

I wish he knew how much I'd love to be there for dinner tonight. And the night after that. But I shake my head. "I'm sorry. I can't."

He laughs, but I can tell that part of him is serious when he asks me. "Why? You have a date or something?"

I shrug as if I'm feeling defeated, and maybe I am a little bit. "What does it matter, Ford? I said this couldn't be serious. I said that nothing could come of it. I don't know what my future holds..."

FORD

I look at her with my heart in my throat. "And I said I wasn't letting you go."

She shrugs in indifference, like she doesn't care that she's breaking my heart right now. "You don't get to choose, Ford. It's my decision what happens. I told you that I didn't want this... that there's things I want... that I need to do. We should never—"

I cut her off. We're standing by where she parked, and I set all the bags on the ground before I box her in against the side of her car. "We should never have what? Made love? Is that what you think?"

She looks so sad for just a minute and then just like that, her expression is blank. She lifts her chin at me. "No, we shouldn't have. You want more than I'm ready to give."

"Bullshit. You're scared, Lily. You're scared of what you're feeling for me and Ollie. I saw you back there. You love that little boy."

She nods, and her heart is in her eyes. "I do. You're right, I do love Ollie, but I shouldn't. I should have protected him because I'm not a good bet, Ford. I told you in the beginning I didn't want this."

I take a deep breath and let it out slowly, trying to catch my breath and keep my cool. I drop my hands from the car and take a step back. I visibly shudder, feeling defeated, and I pace back in forth in front of her. "I don't get it. I just don't get it."

She stands rigidly, her arms crossed over her body. "You don't get what, Ford? What don't you get?"

I stop in front of her, overcome with emotion. "What is it about me that makes people want to walk away from me? Everyone I loved or hell, thought I loved has walked away from me. My mom, my ex-wife. What makes it so damn easy to walk away from me?"

My gaze clouds with tears, and I walk away. I only get a few steps when Lily calls my name. I turn, not even trying to hide the anguish on my face. "You deserve happiness, Lilian. Even if you don't choose me and Ollie, you deserve to be happy and go after what you want. I don't want to hold you back. I want to give you everything you want. But it's up to you now. I can't force you to choose me. To choose us. But hear this—no one will love you like I do, Lilian. If me letting you go makes you happy, I'll do it. Even if it kills me. I just want you to be happy."

I turn back around and walk toward my car. I get in and barely get it started before I'm backing out of the parking spot and pulling out onto the road. I wipe at the damn tear in my eye. For a man that never shows emotion, I sure let it go. But I knew it would happen. If anyone can bring this kind of emotion out of me, it would be Lily.

I drive across town. I pass the office and instead go home. I've put in a full day, and I need a breather before I have to turn around and go pick up Ollie when school ends.

Fuck, a drink would be nice right now to help dull the pain, but I don't have that option. No, I'm going to have to deal with this sober.

LILIAN

I sat in the school parking lot and bawled my eyes out. I tried to control it, but I couldn't. When I was finally able to pull myself together enough to drive home, I went straight to bed. I did finally text my sister back. "I can't make it tonight. I have a work thing but I'll be by this weekend."

After that, I turned my phone off and cried some more.

On Saturday, I got dressed and was going to go talk to Philip and Carrie, but just thinking about Ford and Ollie had me crying all over again. I know when I eventually make it to my sister's house, I need to be supportive, and I need one more day to bury myself in my own misery before I can do that.

By Saturday afternoon, I had put on my sweatpants and a T-shirt. I went through the pictures I took and edited them before I uploaded them to the store in Jasper that does one hour processing.

I drove into Jasper to pick up a gift card for Ollie and a photo album with the printed picture and some wrapping paper. I sat in the parking lot of the store, going through the pictures, pulling out the doubles of the ones I wanted to have a copy of. And then I cried some more.

By Sunday morning, I'm sick of myself and know I need to pull myself together. I turn my phone on and immediately text Carrie and tell her I'm bringing over brunch. I figure I'll go there and then head over to the trampoline park for Ollie's birthday party. Surely by then I can put a smile on my face. I'm going to have to.

I check my email to make sure I haven't missed anything important, and an email from Ford is jumping out at me. I hold my breath and open it, scanning it quickly. After reading it once, I read it again.

"You deserve everything you want out of life. You deserve happiness. All my love, Ford."

I go on to see that he has bought me an opportunity to study two weeks with Aron Roco, a world-renowned photographer based out of New York City. The email contains all the information. Ford has paid for the flight there and lodging. He's taken care of all the details.

I should be happy, but instead I feel almost hollow. He's giving me something I've dreamed about—he's handing it to me—and I'm discovering that it's not really my dream anymore.

All I've thought about since Friday was when Ford asked me why he was so easy to walk away from. Damn, he completely gutted me, and the truth is, it's not easy at all. I need to talk to my sister. I can go with her to help her get moved in and settled, but I will be coming back. I have to because I know when I go, I'll be leaving my heart here.

I put my phone in my cup holder and drive across town. I stop in at Red's Diner and get some breakfast to go and then head to Philip and Carrie's apartment. When I pull in, Carrie's outside, walking her poodle.

"Hey!" she says with a big smile on her face.

I know I probably still look a mess. I can't hide things from her, and my face is blotchy even with the makeup on it. That's why I'm going to get straight to the point.

I grab the food and meet her outside the fence of the dog walking area. "I can't move, Carrie."

She opens her mouth, and I shake my head. "No, hear me out. I can go with you and help you get settled, but I have to come back. I can't leave Ford and Ollie."

Her mouth drops open. "You mean your hot boss and his kid?"

I nod, biting on to my lip. I want to say that they're so much more than that, but I keep my mouth closed, expecting her to be upset.

She tilts her head to the side. "He didn't tell you?"

"He didn't tell me what? Who didn't tell me?"

"Ford! Friday morning he and his brothers met Philip at the distillery plant. He was interviewed by Ford's brothers. They offered him the job on the spot. He gets a company car, he's making more money, and we get to stay in Whiskey Run!"

I hold my hand up. "Wait! Ford didn't interview him?"

She bends down and picks up Fluffy. "No! He told Philip that he would hire him on the spot just to keep us in Whiskey Run. He told him"—she laughs—"he told him that he really needed us to stay in Whiskey Run and to not fuck it up. Isn't that hilarious?"

I nod as my mind goes a million miles a minute. On Friday, at Ollie's school party, he knew. He knew then that Philip and Carrie were staying. So why?

I throw my head back. "Oh God. What have I done?"

She comes at me. "What is it? What's wrong?"

"I fucked up, Carrie. I mean, I really fucked up."

She puts an arm around me. "What did you do?"

I start to cry, and she holds me tightly. Fluffy is freaking out being squashed between us, and she puts him on the ground. "Whatever it is, we can fix it, Lily. What's wrong?"

"When you sent that text, I thought you were telling me you were moving. I thought that you wanted me to go with you to Georgia. I pretty much told Ford that he was a one-night stand and I didn't want to be with him." I pace in the grass. "What did I do?"

Carrie blocks my path, and instead of compassion, there's anger on her face. "Lily, stop and listen to me. I've told you over and over I'm fine. Yeah, I'm a baby sometimes, but only because you're like a mom to me and sometimes I need a mom, but listen. You can't keep doing this. You can't put your life, your dreams, your wants on hold because of me. It's time for you to get what you want now. You deserve it."

I'm nodding my head, knowing she's right. There's fear building up inside me but something else too. I'm excited and eager for what my life could look like. I just have to be brave enough to go after it.

Carrie takes the bag of food from my hand. "Now all you have to do is figure out what you want."

I hug her tightly and then pull back. I look at her, seeing a grown woman in front of me instead of my little sister, and I nod my head. "I have to go. I'm going to get what I want, Carrie. Wish me luck!"

I turn around and jog back to my car.

"What about the food?"

"You and Philip enjoy it. I'll call you later."

"Good luck!" she calls after me.

FORD

The last thing I feel like doing is being on for a party, but there's no way I'm going to let Ollie down. I got here early to set up and decorate a little. I'm not a decorator, but hopefully it's passable. I go out to the car to grab the cake when some other kids show up. The moms all step in to help me, and for the first time I appreciate their butting in.

"Everything looks great!" Tommy's mom says. "I'm sorry you couldn't make it for dinner. I never did get a reply to my text. Maybe we can get together this week."

I shake my head. "I'm sorry, I've been pretty busy with work and everything. If you ever want the boys to play together, I can make that happen."

I point across the room where some of the kids are

gathered around the birthday cake. "I better go and make sure the cake is safe. I'll catch up with you later."

I walk away as fast as and I can, and when I get to Ollie, I can feel the shift in the room. Just like every other time that Lily is around, I feel it. I lift my head and mentally prepare myself to see her. She's standing in the doorway with the camera hanging around her neck, and she has a wrapped present in her hands.

She comes toward us, and Ollie intercepts her. "Lily! You're here! Don't forget we have to play dodgeball and you're going down."

She high-fives him. "I've been looking forward to it all weekend, and you forget it, because if anyone's going down, it's you."

He throws his head back in a laugh, and all his buddies do too. She walks over to the gift table and sets down the present before coming toward me. I can't help it; I'm sure she sees it in my eyes anyway. "You look beautiful."

Her eyes light up, and I realize now that she's closer, her eyes are a little puffy as if she's been crying. I'm about to ask her about it when the party coordinator comes in. "Okay, so who's ready to jump?"

The kids all start screaming and jumping up and down.

She calms them down. "Okay so first we jump for

an hour. Then we're going to come back in here and eat some cake, and Ollie—the birthday boy—is going to open presents, okay?"

They all cheer and nod their heads. She goes over a few rules with them, and then they're all on their way. I want to talk to Lily, but Ollie is pulling her out the door.

The parents all follow behind. My dad and stepmom are here. Lucas and Issi, Beau and Austin are all here too. I look at Beau. "Where's Natalie?"

He shrugs without looking at me. "She's sorry she couldn't make it. She sends her love, and she sent a present for Ollie."

"But—" I start, and finally Beau looks at me. "Please, not now, Ford. I can't talk about it now."

I nod my head and cross my arms over my chest. All eyes are on the kids playing dodgeball. Instead of Lily being on opposite teams of Ollie, she was the first person he picked for his team. They laugh, give each other fist-bumps, and she keeps the kids laughing with all her antics.

My family is all gathered around when Lucas clears his throat. "I know it's not necessarily the best place for this, but Issi and I have an announcement."

My parents and brothers all turn to them, and I know what they're going to say before they even say it.

They both have pure happiness on their faces. Lucas holds his hands up in the air. "We're pregnant! We're going to have a baby."

We all take turns hugging Issi and slapping a proud Lucas on the back. Even with all the shit I have going on, I can't help but be happy for them. They deserve this.

The other parents are all looking at us, no doubt wondering what's going on, and Issi tells one of the other moms and they all offer their congratulations too.

The hour goes by quickly, and I'm waiting on the sidelines when the kids come off the mats. I hand Lily a cold bottle of water. The kids have not let her sit down one time. Her face is red and flushed, and she's panting, but she looks like she's having a good time. Fuck, I'm going to miss her. My heart is breaking, and it sucks acting like it's not.

We walk side by side back to the party room. The kids and parents are all in front of us, and I know I shouldn't be back here. I don't trust myself not to beg her to stay with me.

"Thanks for getting Philip the job."

I shrug. "He was the perfect candidate for it."

Before we go through the door of the room, she stops and puts her hand on my arm. I have no strength to resist her, and her touching me is not helping matters. "Thank you for the gift too. It's too much."

Before I tell her she deserves it, she asks me, "Will you be mad if I don't take it? At least not anytime soon?"

I search her face. "No. I won't be mad."

She nods. "Good. I don't want to leave."

She doesn't say why, but I can guess. "Because your sister is staying in Whiskey Run now?"

She shakes her head. "No, because you and Ollie are here. I don't want to leave either one of you."

She holds her hand up and takes a step toward me, pressing her body to mine. "Don't get me wrong. I want to learn to take pictures, but I can take classes online or at the college in Jasper. I want to travel and see the world, but I can do that a few weeks out of the year when Ollie's on winter or summer break."

I hold my breath, needing her to spell it out for me. "What does that mean, Lilian?"

"You need to know that I can't walk away from you, Ford. I couldn't do it. Before I knew about Philip's job, I talked to my sister and told her I would help her get settled, but I wasn't leaving you and Ollie." She takes a deep breath and nervously says, "I love you, Ford. I love you and Ollie. I want to date you, and I don't want to hide what we have between us. I know I hurt you Friday, and I promise I'll make it up to you."

I grip on to her shoulders. "You love me?"

She bites her lip and nods.

I lift her up in my arms and spin her around. I kiss her until we're both breathless.

My brother Lucas pokes his head out of the party room. "Ford, Lily! We're about to sing happy birthday."

I let Lily slide down my body and grab her hand. "We'll finish this later."

We walk back into the party hand in hand. Issi is lighting candles, and when she sees us come in the door, she winks at Lily and starts singing "Happy Birthday." Both Lily and I sing along and watch as Ollie basks in being the center of attention. Lily takes pictures trying to capture it all. Ollie blows out the candles way before he should, but I don't even care. Lily loves me, and that's all I can focus on right now.

The kids devour the cake, and then Ollie starts opening presents. He likes the gift card that Lily got him, but he loves the pictures that she had printed from his school party. He flips through the book and comes over to Lily. She squats down on one knee, taking in his serious expression. "What's wrong, Ollie?"

He shrugs, holding up the picture album. "I love this, but there's not any pictures of me and you."

Lily puts her hand to her chest, right over her heart. Her voice is thick when she asks him. "Do you want a picture of me and you?"

He nods, and Lily pulls the camera off her shoulder and hands it to Issi. "Will you take a picture of Ollie and me?"

She nods and points the camera at them as Lily wraps her arms around Ollie. They both smile and then make a funny face before Ollie looks up at me. "Now the three of us. Come on, Dad."

I get down on one knee and wrap my arms around both of them. Who knew that today would work out like this and I'd be holding my whole heart in my arms?

The party is a complete hit, and as we're cleaning up and piling everything into my car, Ollie is going on and on about how it was the best birthday party ever.

"I agree it was the best birthday party ever, but now it's time for a nap."

Ollie is shocked. "A nap? I'm six now. I don't nap."

Lily laughs next to us, and Ollie grabs her hand. "Dad, can Lily come over to our house?"

I open my car door for Ollie to get in and look at Lily hopefully. "That's up to Lily."

She nods. "I'd love to come over." She leans down

to look through the car door. "But that depends. Are you going to call me old if I take a little nap?"

I put my hand to her back as Ollie shakes his head. "You're not old. You can take a nap at our house."

She raises up. "Is that okay with you, Ford?"

I lean in, and her eyes widen as I kiss her. I don't know if she thought I was going to break it in slowly with Ollie or what, but I'm not. I want the world to know that she's ours.

She looks at Ollie to see his reaction, and he just keeps smiling at Lily and me. I lean in and whisper to her, "Is nap code for something else?"

She puts her hand on my chest and whispers back, "As long as I'm in your arms, it can be code for whatever you want it to be."

LILIAN

I pick up the phone, knowing that it's Ford calling me from his office. "Can I see you in my office, Lilian?"

I try to keep the smile off my face, but I can't. "Sure thing, boss. I'll be right there."

I look over at our new hire, Elle, and she's busy entering last week's delivery numbers. She's proven to be a good hire, and I'm so glad that Lucas took a chance on her. She's a hard worker. "Elle, Ford needs me. I'll be right back."

She smiles at me. "Sure, I got the phone." No sooner does she get the words out than she's looking back down at her computer screen.

I grab a pad of paper and a pen off my desk and go

to Ford's office. I knock on his open door, and he waves me in.

I get into the room, and he points to the hard wood behind me. "Shut the door, please."

My nether regions start to tingle as I shut the door. He's sitting at his desk, looking all calm. He has his hands folded together on the desk in front of him.

I stand awkwardly, and he points to the chair that I usually sit in.

My cheeks heat, and I go to sit down. I'm here to work. I don't know why I thought he would be calling me in here for something else. "So this week you have appointments with Axle Distributing, and then Caro Distributing is sending one of their people on Thursday. Then Friday, you go to North Carolina to meet with Mountain Moonshine. Ollie has a night game on Saturday, so you may be able to make it back in time for that."

He's nodding his head, but he's not with me. He seems to have his mind on something else. "Is that it?" he asks.

I nod and then stomp down the nerves I'm feeling. This is Ford. I need to just say it. "Actually, I was hoping to talk to you about something, but it's personal, so if you feel like this is not a good time, I can wait until tonight."

His jaw tightens, and he encourages me with only a nod. The loving Ford from last night seems to have vanished in this suit and tie. I sit up a little taller and pull my shoulders back. "Yeah, well, I thought since you were going out of town, you could let Ollie stay with me." I hold my hand up before he says anything. "I know that your brothers take turns watching him, but they have their own lives. If he stayed with me, I could focus on him. We could hang out, and I could make sure he's rested for his game. I'd make sure he's there an hour before it starts like he's supposed to be."

He's watching me with no expression. He gets up from his chair and comes around to sit on the edge of his desk right in front of me. "Are you sure you want to do that? You know that you don't have to."

Now I'm starting to get pissed. He acts like I can't handle it or something. "I mean if you don't trust me or want me to hang out with Ollie then just say so—"

He pulls me out of my chair so quickly, I drop the pen and paper in my hands. My body slams against his, and he has his hands at my back, holding me flush against him. "Of course I trust you with Ollie. I want you to hang out with him. But I don't want to force you. I don't ever want you to feel like I'm holding you back or forcing you into something you don't want to do. I've tried to give you your space."

I let out a breath. "Is that what this is, Ford? Is that what you've been doing? All the hot and cold, wanting me one second and pushing me away the next?"

"I always want you. Don't doubt that. But yeah, I don't want you to feel like I'm trying to take over your life."

I bring my hand up and cup his cheek. "Ford, you don't get it. You and Ollie are my life. I choose you always... and you don't hold me back. You encourage me all the time. The camera... the classes with Aron that are scheduled this summer..." I snap my fingers. "You're the one that encouraged me to start taking pictures at all the soccer games. People want to buy the pictures I take. They want to pay money!" I say in amazement.

He rocks me side to side with pride on his face. "Because you're that good."

I slide my hands to his chest. "None of that matters, though. You and Ollie are what matter."

He lets out a breath and leans down, pressing his forehead to mine, and his voice breaks with emotion. "Thank God."

I pull back and look at him, searching his eyes. "Ford? What is it? What's wrong?"

His hands tighten on me as if he's afraid to let me go. "I can't keep doing things this way. I'm tired of waking up and you being gone. I want you next to me when I go to bed at night and when I wake up in the morning. I always want you with me."

My hands curl against his chest, and my breath comes out in little pants. "What are you saying?"

He releases me then, shaking his head. "Please don't let me fuck this up." He walks around to his side of the desk, pulls something out of the drawer, and walks back to me holding out a little blue box in his palm. "I love you, Lilian. I love you more than I ever thought possible. I've had this ring since before we went to Vegas when you told me you were going to start dating. I knew then that I loved you and wanted you as my wife." He drops down to one knee. "I love you, baby. If you'll do me the honor of being my wife, I promise to love you always, to always put your needs above my own, and to help you reach all your dreams. Will you marry me, Lily?"

I go down to my knees on the soft carpet and wrap my arms around him. "Yes, yes, I'll marry you."

He puts the ring on my finger, but I barely look at it. "I love you and Ollie, Ford. I will never, ever walk away from either of you."

He exhales a long sigh. "If you tried, I'd come after you."

I pull at the buttons of his shirt and slide my hands against his hard chest. "So now we celebrate?"

"Now we celebrate." He presses his lips to mine and makes me his in every sense of the word.

Epilogue
Ford

"All right, let's get to it."

I try to give the guys my serious, *let's get down to business* face, but I can't stop smiling.

Austin looks at me. "What's that look?"

Lucas rolls his eyes. "I'm sure I know what he's smiling about. Anyone that was near his office this morning will know why he's smiling."

I should be upset that Lily and I were a little loud. It's not very professional for the CEO of the company to be heard having a good time behind closed doors, but I can't be upset about it because she said yes. Lilian said yes.

"Whatever, Lucas. It's not like I haven't caught you and Issi in your office."

Beau, always the serious one, interrupts. "Guys, you can't use Blaze Distillery offices for your little trysts. There are rules and policies…"

Austin is smiling ear to ear. "Fuck, Beau, let them have a good time. Lucas is married, and Ford has stopped being a dick. Let him have his fun."

Beau takes his glasses off, folds them up, and sets them on the table in front of him. "Exactly, Lucas is married. Ford is having—"

I point at him with a stern look. "Watch what you say…"

Beau smiles tightly and continues. "Ford is engaging in inappropriate behavior with an employee. His assistant, for crying out loud. This is a lawsuit waiting—"

I laugh. I can't help it. I laugh out loud before leaning forward. All eyes are on me, and I no longer care that I'm smiling like some fool. "I asked Lily to marry me, and she said yes."

There's a collective gasp around the table, and then they all are out of their seats giving me hugs and pats on the back.

"I can't believe she said yes to you, you old bastard," Austin says, slapping me on the back as he gives me a tight hug.

Lucas is next. "Congratulations, brother. I'm so happy for you."

Beau is happy for me but a little reserved. "Congratulations big brother. I'm happy for you."

Everyone is talking at once when our phones all ding at the same time. The only time that happens is when we get a message from our group text. We all pull our phones out and read them simultaneously.

"I'm coming home."

The message from Huddy has us all a little bit emotional. We each respond, and I text to him, "I can't wait to see you, brother."

We have so much to celebrate. Lilian said yes... and my brother is coming home.

Want to read Hudson's story?
Get it in Coming Home.

Want more of Whiskey Run?

Whiskey Run

Faithful - He's the hot, say-it-like-it-is cowboy, and he won't stop until he gets the woman he wants.

Captivated - She's a beautiful woman on the run... and I'm going to be the one to keep her.

Obsessed - She's loved him since high school and now he's back.

Seduced - He's a football player that falls in love with the small town girl.

Devoted - She's a plus size model and he's a small town mechanic.

Whiskey Run: Savage Ink

Virile - He won't let her go until he puts his mark on her.

Torrid - He'll do anything to give her what she wants.

Rigid - If you love reading about emotionally wounded men and the women that help them overcome their past, then you'll love Dawson and Emily's story.

Whiskey Run: Cowboys Love Curves

Obsessed Cowboy - She's the preacher's daughter and she's

off limits.

Whiskey Run: Heroes

Ransom - He's on a mission he can't lose.

Redeem - He's in love with his sister's best friend.

Submit - She's his fake wife but he wants to make it real.

Forbid - They have a secret romance but he's about to stake his claim.

Whiskey Run: Sugar

One Night Love - Her one night stand wants more.

Rebound Love - She's falling for the rebound guy.

Second Chance Love - He is not a man to ignore... especially when he asks for a second chance.

Bad Boy Love - He's a bad boy that wants her good.

Whiskey Run: Guardians MC

Protective Biker - She needs his protection and he'll give it to her. But he's going to need her heart in exchange.

Broken Biker - There's only one woman for him...

Relentless Biker - He won't stop until he has her back.

JOIN ME!

JOIN MY NEWSLETTER

www.AuthorHopeFord.com/Subscribe

Be a Hottie!

JOIN HOPE'S HOTTIES ON FACEBOOK

www.FB.com/groups/hopeford

A place to talk about Hope Ford's books! Find out about new releases, giveaways, get exclusive content, see covers before anyone else and more!

About the Author

USA Today Bestselling Author Hope Ford writes short, steamy, sweet romances. She loves tattooed, alpha men, instant love stories, and ALWAYS happily ever afters. She has over 100 books and they are all available on Amazon.

To find me on Pinterest, Instagram, Facebook, Goodreads, and more:

www.AuthorHopeFord.com/follow-me

Want FREE BOOKS?
Go to www.authorhopeford.com/freebies